D1629717

FIELD OF THE FORTY FOOTSTEPS

The children of Wapping jeered at her hair—"As red as raspberry jam". During her early years she had no name but Child, and her guardian was 'Aunt'. The sordid alley tavern was more prison than home to the nameless girl, and the shadowy figure called Peter, reputedly Aunt's husband, became a threat to her life as well as to her freedom.

When Child learned she had four names, Marie Annette Madeleine Veronique, the mystery of her parenthood deepened. Why were they French names? And where was her mother's letter, the only clue to her birth?

Not until she was seventeen did she experience a dramatic change in her life. Her cousin Alain rescued her and carried her off to Rippiers, a country mansion outside the ancient Cinque Port of Rye.

But even there, amidst the unfamiliar luxury, she found herself threatened, and as she began to solve the puzzle of the field of forty footsteps, so the danger swelled like the great globe of Alain's balloon. There seemed no one she could trust, and the balloon itself became, instead of a pleasure vessel, a weapon designed to destroy her.

FIELD OF THE
FORTY FOOTSTEPS

by

PHYLLIS HASTINGS

St. Martin's Press
NEW YORK

Robert Hale Limited
LONDON

ISBN 0 7091 7072 6

Robert Hale Limited
Clerkenwell House
Clerkenwell Green
London, EC1R 0HT

First published in the United States of America in 1979

Library of Congress Cataloging in Publication Data

Hastings, Phyllis, 1913–
    Field of forty footsteps.

    I. Title.
PZ4.H358Fh 1979 [PR6058.A82] 823′.9′14 78–19446
ISBN 0–312–28825–5

Printed in Great Britain
by Billing & Sons Limited, Guildford, London and Worcester

PART ONE

Wapping

ONE

Almost soundlessly the boat slid up the river, cleaving the water as though it had been oil. The two oarsmen paid no heed to the trailing, uncertain drift of mist, or to the nervous fog-horns of ships announcing their positions. They handled their little boat with no more concern than if they had been circumnavigating a village pond.

The solitary passenger sat facing them from the stern, holding a bundle upon his knees. He made no attempt at conversation, but neither Tom Stitch nor Jimmy, his son, felt the lack of this. Night jobs were not infrequent for men who knew the river, and who knew how to keep quiet and forget what they had seen and where they had been. With foreign ships anchored in the estuary there was a fair traffic in folk wanting to enter the country or leave it without drawing attention to themselves.

This particular fare was a Frenchman. Tom was old enough to remember when the Frenchies were enemies, and he scowled to himself. Fight 'em or kiss 'em, a man didn't know where he was. Still, the promised pay was good, and in these days the Thames watermen were hard hit, with so many bridges, and now those evil-smelling steam-boats belching black smoke and stirring up the river in a way it was never intended to be stirred.

The rhythmic movement of the rowing lulled Tom into a state which was not far from a light doze. This did not trouble him, for he knew he could depend on Jimmy to keep them headed in the right direction, but suddenly he was startled by a sound. There was nothing strident or alarming about it. It was, in fact, as gentle as the bleat of a new-born lamb. The surprising thing was that it came from the bundle.

"O crimes!" Tom exclaimed. "What was that?"

The Frenchman answered him. "It is a baby."

Tom knew it was not his business to ask questions, but this was an unprecedented occurrence, a mystery beyond his powers of solving. If the foreigner wished to be rid of the child, why go to so much trouble? The water was there, waiting, and who would make a fuss about such a small bundle? If, on the other hand, he wished to preserve it, why expose it to the dangers of a foggy night on the Thames?

"Yours?" It seemed as safe a question as any, but the Frenchman did not reply, and they continued in silence.

At Wapping Old Stairs they drew into the darker shadows and tied up and disembarked. The Frenchman handed over the agreed amount of money and then said, "Please to direct me to an ale-house that is called, I think, The Leather Bottle."

The Stitches knew it well, as they knew all thirty-six taverns in Wapping High Street and Wapping Wall, but Jimmy saw fit to say, "They'll be abed, you know. They don't sit up all night."

The Frenchman nodded, murmured, "I thank you," and turned and walked away.

The Leather Bottle was situated in an alley off the High Street. It was by no means an elegant building, being low and squat, and some subsidence in its foundations had caused it to lean slightly awry, so that it had the appearance of sinking into the ground, as a gravestone might do.

The Frenchman tried the door which, as he had expected, was bolted. He hesitated to knock, for fear of arousing the neighbours, but there was no alternative, especially as the baby was now producing a small yet shrill cry. He rapped gently with his knuckles, once, twice, three times, without effect, then in despair used the full force of his fist.

A window above his head was thrown open. "Who's that?" shouted a female voice. "What d'you want? Blazes! I can't hear a word you say. And I can't see you. It's as dark as Newgate knocker. Go away!"

The window was slammed shut, and the Frenchman was forced to knock once more.

This time the bolts were drawn back and the door opened. The woman stood before him with a candlestick in her hand.

"Leave us alone!" She spoke more quietly, but her voice was fierce. "My husband's upstairs. He'll bash you if he comes down."

"Please to allow me to enter."

"A foreigner!" She sounded even more angry and dismayed. "A fine reputation you'll give us. No, you shan't come in, and if you need a drink, the river's just down the street."

As though it had been given a cue, the baby began to wail again.

"What's that?" the woman snapped.

"What like is the sound?" the Frenchman asked, wearily.

"Oh, come in!" She indicated that he should be seated, then put down the candle and went to a barrel from which she filled a mug.

"Drink that and be gone! Oh, give me the child while you're supping. You hold it like it was a bundle of dirty clothes."

The Frenchman looked relieved. "With you it will be better." Quickly he drank, then stood up and made for the door.

"Hi! Cut that!" the woman cried. "Where do you think you're going?"

"My business is finished. I deliver the baby. Good!"

"Oh, no, you don't! If you think you can foist some poor little bastard on me—"

With a swift movement she interposed herself between him and the door. "Now you take this brat and be off."

"No. I bring it from France. For you."

"But—"

"The letter. Almost I forget. Here." He drew it, crumpled,

from his pocket and pushed it inside the child's shawl, as though it were a price tag.

Mary Hay stared at him. Something was moving in her mind, a suspicion, a belief she wanted to deny, a truth she wanted to disown.

"Whose baby is this?" she asked.

"It is the child of your sister."

"Is she—"

"She is well. She send the baby with me because she has fear. She will follow. Soon she will come."

Mary sighed. "She always was crazy. What is she afraid of now?"

"There is another revolution. It is small, but revolution it is."

"I am supposed to look after the child until she arrives?"

"The child of your sister," the Frenchman repeated. "Please!"

She moved away from the door and he was gone before she could speak again. Where he would lodge, where he would go, whether he would return to France or would remain among those refugees who appeared mysteriously whenever the word 'revolution' was breathed, these things she did not know, and had no concern with them. All that mattered was that a stranger had brought a tiny living human being and made her responsible for it, she who was a childless woman with no time or liking for children. She gazed at the small, puckered face, and she was disturbed and afraid.

TWO

The child thrived, as the unwanted sometimes do. Those on whom love is lavished may slip away, almost as though an excess of love weakens them, while those who must depend upon themselves grow up sturdy and self-reliant.

It was not that the child was neglected. She was fed adequately and she was kept clean, but as she passed from babyhood to little-girlhood, she came to know the loneliness for which she had no word, only a feeling of emptiness, of hands wanting to hold something which was not there.

The room in which she spent most of her time was in the upper storey, away from the society of the tavern, and as soon as she had grown tall enough she would spend hours looking down on the world which moved beneath her window, and came thus to know that horses and dogs existed, going on four legs, and that people, while coming in many shapes and sizes, consisted of two main groups, those whose legs were forked and those who were shrouded from the waist down. She longed to make contact with the passers-by, wave to them or call out, but the window was kept closed, in case she should fall from it, and so the panorama below remained a picture, scarcely more real than her dreams.

Two people were solid and substantial to her. One of them was dressed in skirts and was called Aunt. The other wore trousers and was called Peter. She knew, as early as she had understanding, that Peter resented her presence; knew it by the surly manner and the reluctance to speak to her or to answer if she spoke.

Aunt was different. Aunt had hair as shiny as the brass on

the harness of the horses, as bright as the sun which for one brief hour in the day managed to elude the chimneys and the gables and the signboards and creep through the windows of The Leather Bottle. Aunt was pretty, but she was difficult to love, because she was busy.

'Child' was all that Aunt ever called her, and so she believed it to be her name. At that time her vocabulary was extremely limited, through lack of communication with others, and Mary Hay began to harbour the suspicion that the child was simple.

"What have I loaded myself with, an idiot?"

"More fool you!" Peter sneered. "That sister of yours has made you her ape all right. Reckon she never did intend to come for the kid."

"Then we'll have to put up with it, won't we?"

"Or get rid of it."

"How?"

"I'd find a way."

"You're jealous."

"What! Of a beef-headed little bastard that isn't worth the food she sops up?"

"Are you worth your keep?"

"If that's how you feel, I know what to do."

Mary Hay caught Peter's arm. "I didn't mean it. Truly I didn't. You can't go. How can you?"

"Oh, stop your snivelling! And keep the whelp out of my way, if you know what's good for it and for you."

Mary was only too glad to obey. An ale-house such as the Leather Bottle, frequented by sailors, watermen, coster-mongers, street-sellers of all kinds, vagrants, thieves and worse than thieves, was no place for a child. The public rooms, therefore, were forbidden, and because of this rule they came to represent, for Child, a paradise from which she was shut out.

Once, greatly tempted by singing voices, she descended the stairs and stood by the door leading to the bar. There Mary found her, and scolded her, striking her and driving her up the stairs to bed, but later, remorseful, she said to Peter, "Poor little brat! She has a dull time."

Peter grunted. "I've told you often enough. This is no place for her."

"Well, as she is here, we do have some responsibility."

"I don't."

"Please yourself. I say she can't be kept a prisoner in that room for ever. She'll grow into a puny wench. She doesn't even get any fresh air. I shall take her for a walk every day. Well, most days."

"And who's to look after this place?"

"Why not you?"

"Now you know how I feel about mixing with the crowd."

"Well, you can't hide among the barrels for the rest of your life. They've accepted you now."

"I don't think we should draw attention to ourselves. They'll wonder whose kid it is."

Mary laughed. "Maybe they'll think it's ours."

"Sometimes," Peter said, viciously, "I could kill you."

At first Child was terrified of going into the streets. She clung to Aunt's hand and whimpered and begged to be taken home, but gradually she overcame her fear.

Sometimes Aunt took her to the shops or the market, sometimes she stopped to talk to acquaintances, and Child, starved as she was of knowledge and human contact, lapped up the conversations and the idle gossip, learning late the simple everyday things that most children pick up from the cradle.

"Are you my mother?"

"Of course not! You know perfectly well I'm your aunt."

"And Peter isn't my father?"

"No."

"Well, what is an aunt?"

"An aunt is a mother's sister."

It took Child a few minutes to work this out. "If you are my aunt, then I must have a mother."

Aunt hesitated. "It doesn't always follow."

"Is my mother dead?"

"I don't know. I haven't seen her since—not for a long time."

"If she's not dead, why isn't she here?"

Mary Hay was not given to overmuch sentiment, but now a pang of pity pierced her. Poor mite! What kind of a life lay before her?

"One day, Child, when you're older, I'll tell you about it. You were brought here when you were a baby, and your mother wrote a letter saying she would follow later."

"But she hasn't come," Child said, dolefully.

"No. Not yet."

"Not yet." Dismay turned to excitement. "She will come. Perhaps tomorrow." She skipped for joy. "She'll come tomorrow. She will, won't she, Aunt?

Mary hadn't the heart to quench that liveliness. Why, the child was quite a bright little thing when she was roused. So she replied, evasively, "Perhaps."

Now there was an added zest to their outings, and as they passed through the streets Child would look intently into the faces of the women, in case one of them might be her mother. She spent hours at the window of her little room, for there was a definite purpose in scrutinizing the people who went up and down the alley. But gradually, as time brought no result, hope faded and she became lethargic. What was the use of expecting someone who never came?

To her aunt she said, flatly, "She's dead, you know."

Aunt, startled, for a moment did not understand. "Who is?"

"My mother."

"Why should you think that?"

"I'm not a baby now," Child told her, scornfully. "Mother would have come if she'd been alive."

To Peter Mary Hay said, "The child will have to go to school. I can't have her growing up plumb ignorant."

"Reckon you'll be sending her to a dame-school with the quality," Peter sneered.

"No, and I'm not sending her to the penny-a-week Red Lion either."

"Then let her be."

"And have everybody put upon her? Give her no chance to do anything but go on the streets? She'll soon be a young lady. But perhaps you wouldn't notice a thing like that. She needs company. She's been real mumpish lately."

Most people, Mary reflected, would have put the brat into an orphanage, the proper place for unwanted children. She had been soft, and now it was late to turn the girl away.

The thought of education stuck in her mind, and each example of Child's ignorance and innocence was a pinprick. If only the business could be arranged at little or no cost to herself! And as if Heaven approved the quality of her intention, it offered her the opportunity to translate it into a deed.

There was a blind old man, well known in the district, both for his usefulness and his eccentricity. He was a parson without a living, or so it was said, for everyone called him "Reverend". His usefulness consisted of his work as a scrivener. Few sailors possessed sufficient learning to sit down and pen a letter to absent families, and when their ships put in at London docks they would seek out the Reverend and pay him to transcribe the messages they wished to send.

Sailors are not generally miserly, and the Reverend could have lived in some little comfort but for his eccentricity, which was to wander from one to another of the street markets and buy all the singing-birds he could afford. There were linnets, woodlarks, goldfinches, greenfinches, nightingales, and the more common thrushes and blackbirds. These birds were popular commodities, for as well as being musical pets in private households they were contestants in the singing-matches, on which a considerable amount of money was wagered. Some when captured were blinded, this being claimed to improve their song, and of these the Reverend wrung the necks, as quickly and mercifully as possible. The others he set free.

Mary Hay made inquiries and soon learned where the Reverend was to be found. His home consisted of a room in a house chiefly occupied by dock-labourers, and the room was bare save for a table, one chair, and what seemed to Mary to be a large and surely an unnecessary quantity of books.

He offered her the chair, and she told him the reason for her visit. "You see, Reverend, it's my niece—"

"I have a name," he interrupted, somewhat testily.

"Everybody calls you Reverend."

"They are not very good at pronouncing words. But I am sure you, mistress, will have no difficulty. I am John Cooperthwayte."

"That's a proper mouthful," she said, in wonder. "And are you just Mister, the same as everybody else?"

"Yes, I am like others, except that I have lost my sight."

"Well, my niece, she's bright enough, but that ignorant you wouldn't believe it. She's a big girl, ten years going on eleven, and she can't read nor write."

"Why doesn't she go to school?"

"Because I won't send her to the ragged school, and I can't afford for her to mix with the gentry. Will you come and give her lessons, Reverend—Mr Cooper—um?"

The old man did not reply immediately, and Mary added, "I can't pay you anything. But you'll get a meal every day, a good hot meal, meat and potatoes, with bread and cheese if you want it, and a mug of ale."

Mr Cooperthwayte inclined his head. "Yes, mistress, I will come and teach your niece."

A door was opened for Child, a door to the whole world, but at first she could not see this. She saw only an old man in a rusty black robe, with a shapeless black hat sitting like a crow upon his white head.

"First you shall learn to read," he said, severely, "and then you shall learn to write. I shall not be able to see the quality of your calligraphy, so I shall have to obtain another opinion.

When you are able to read, you can read aloud from my books, and then, only then, can I begin to educate you."

Half-heartedly Child began to struggle with letters and then with words. In turn she became tired, bored, discouraged. She felt she would never master the art. Occasionally she would rebel, flinging down the book. She even went so far as to shout, "I hate you!"

Mr Cooperthwayte was not disturbed by these demonstrations. "Your feelings for me are of no interest," he said coldly. "Hate me if you like, but hate books and you are a fool."

Gradually she began to appreciate her own ignorance, to take an interest in her lessons, to ask questions, and her change of attitude rendered everything more simple. Whenever she came upon a word she did not know, she spelled it out to her teacher, and he told her its pronunciation and meaning. In this way they progressed rapidly, and when less than a year had passed he declared her ready for promotion.

"I have shown your copybook to a friend of mine, and he tells me you write a fair hand. Your reading of English is fluent, so I consider you are ready to begin the Latin tongue."

Child made a sound like a small groan, and Mr Cooperthwayte asked, a little querulously, "Do you not wish to learn Latin?"

"Oh, yes! But please could I not study French as well?"

Mr Cooperthwayte belonged to the old school of classical scholars. "Why French?" he wanted to know.

"Because I was brought from France when I was a baby. Aunt told me. Don't you know French, Reverend?"

"Of course I do!" He was slightly offended at the question. "And I asked you not to address me as Reverend."

"I can't help it. It's quicker. Besides," she added, logically, "you call me Child."

"How very remiss of me! Especially as you are scarcely a child now. What is your name?"

"I don't know."

He stared at her. "You do not know your name? Why, this is preposterous."

"I thought Child was my name," she confessed, "until I could read and found a child could be any boy or girl."

"Have you not asked your aunt?"

"Once or twice. But she says, 'Cut that!' And if I keep on she tells me, 'None of yer lip!' "

"You have a right to know."

His words strengthened her. She went to her aunt. "I want to know my name, my real name. Mr Cooperthwayte says it's time I did."

Mary Hay raised no objection. She merely looked tired and peevish. "All right. You had to know sometime, I suppose, though a lot of good it will do you. Your name is Marie Annette Madeleine Veronique."

THREE

Four names. She said them over and over again, stumbling at first but continuing until all the syllables rolled smoothly from her tongue. Four names. What wealth! What a treasure for a child who had had so little! Four elegant, noble, foreign names. Marie Annette Madeleine Veronique. At first she could not decide which to take for general use. Veronique was romantic. Madeleine sounded genteel. Annette had an air of worldly wisdom and fun. But she came to the conclusion that Marie held all the virtues.

Child stood in front of her mirror and discarded for ever the name by which she had been called. Marie. The looking-glass was so small that she could not see her body. She judged it to be well-shaped, but had had no opportunity to compare it with another unclothed female form. Her face was small, oval rather than round, with large eyes of a blue so dark as to resemble the grey of storm clouds rather than the clear sky of a summer's day. Her hair was red. Sometimes the alley children made fun of it. "Red as raspberry jam," they termed it, but it was nearer the tint of old, much-polished mahogany.

"Why didn't you tell me my name before?" she demanded. "Why did you keep it from me all these years?"

Aunt stared in front of her, as if trying to solve a problem to which she did not know the answer. She was different, Marie realised, with some surprise, had altered in a way hard to define. It was as though she had lost hope, had no more spirit to fight. At last she said, "I expected your mother. I expected I'd have to keep you no more'n a few months.

Then, afterwards, well, it was a cranky name for a Wapping kid."

"How did I get here, when I was a baby?"

"A man brought you."

"Who was he?"

"How should I know?" Aunt asked, irritably. "He was someone your mother could trust. That's all."

"But he told you my name."

"No. It was in the letter."

"The letter?" Excitement surged through Marie. "What letter?"

"The letter your mother sent with you."

"Show it to me! Oh, Aunt, you must let me see it. It's mine. Please don't—"

"Hold your tongue! You're that bounceful anybody would think you'd come into a fortune 'stead of a string of useless names. I can't give you the letter because I haven't got it."

"You didn't throw it away!"

"No, I didn't. I kept it safe, as I thought, but it disappeared."

"How could it? Where did it go?"

"I don't know." Mary rubbed her hand across her forehead. "Don't pester me! My head aches. Things get lost in the end. Everything gets lost, sometime or other."

"But you remember what was in it." Marie clasped her hands together so tightly that the knuckles shone like ivory. "Please! You couldn't forget what my mother wrote."

"I can't recollect hardly anything, and that's a fact. There was what you were called, and that she'd be coming to England soon, and then there was a lot about the trouble in Paris, and—oh, all kinds of stuff that was highfaluting and nonsensical. She'd a great imagination, had our Jane."

"Jane? Was that my mother's name?" Marie's voice tailed off in disappointment.

"Yes. Mary and Jane we was called. Our parents were practical people."

"What about my family name?"

"Family name?" Aunt lost her temper. "What family name?" she inquired, scornfully. "You got no family. You may give yourself airs because you've come into some fancy names, but you're nought but a poor little bastard that's lucky to have a home and three good meals a day. You've been a millstone round my neck, living on charity, but you're well-nigh growed up now and you'll have to go out to work, else help me in the bar. I shall tell the Reverend there's been enough of this education lark."

Mary went away, stricken. Aunt was right. She was a nothing, a nobody. She would never find her relatives, never know who she really was.

Now she had little interest in anything. Mr Cooperthwayte still visited her, for Aunt appeared to have forgotten her threat to dismiss him. Indeed, Aunt was daily becoming more vague and her face was white and drawn, as though she suffered pain. When Marie at last noticed this, her conscience pricked her.

She decided to speak to Peter of the matter though she was somewhat reluctant to do so. Throughout her childhood Peter had been a shadowy figure from whom she had sensed hostility towards herself. Whenever Aunt had suggested anything of benefit to the child, Peter had been quick and forceful with objections, and when speaking to the child, which was rarely, had a brusque, rough manner.

But Aunt's condition was deteriorating. Of this Marie was sure, and was convinced that something must be done about it.

She said, "Aunt must have a doctor."

"What for?" Peter asked, casually.

"She's ill. Haven't you noticed?"

"There's not much wrong with her."

"She has headaches."

"So do most women."

"Fetch a doctor. Then we'll know."

"She wouldn't like that."

"It doesn't matter what she likes. It's what's best for her."

"I know what's best for her."

"Won't you have a doctor, then?"

"No."

"Well, if you won't, I will."

Peter's hand shot out and closed round her wrist, holding it so tightly that she gave a little cry of pain.

"You'll mind your own business. Getting above yourself ain't you, miss?"

Marie was frightened. Unfriendly Peter had been, but had never before given this impression of violence. She decided to wait a little while, in the hope that her aunt might recover naturally, but there was no improvement, and often the headaches were so severe that she was unable to go down to serve her customers, but was obliged to keep to her bed.

One morning Marie awoke suddenly at an unusually early hour. It was full daylight, being early summer, and there was already a bustling and a going to and fro in the alley.

These familiar sounds would not have disturbed her. It was something else which wakened her, a cry of pain, a cry of human pain.

She listened and it came again, from close behind her. The walls of the old tavern were no more than lath and plaster, and the room adjoining hers was that occupied by Mary and Peter.

Swiftly she slipped out of bed and ran into the next room. Mary lay moaning, twisting her head from side to side in an attempt to ease the unbearable pain. But, frightened and anxious though she was, Marie did no more than cast a fleeting glance at her aunt. Her eyes were rivetted on the person known as Peter.

Peter was beside Mary, and was sitting up, naked to the waist. As Marie looked, Peter snatched up the bedclothes to hide the betraying figure, but it was too late.

"You are a woman!" Marie cried. There was no mistaking the conformation of those breasts. Now she wondered why she had not sooner realised. Peter whose face was smooth. Peter who had never been seen to wield a razor. Peter who stayed in the shadows and was uncommunicative, who mingled so rarely with the customers.

Peter sat silent, glaring at Marie from over the blanket. Mary was crying pitifully, and Marie wrenched her attention from her strange discovery.

"Now we must fetch a doctor."

"No!"

"How can you be so cruel?" Marie demanded. "Don't you care what happens to her?"

"Yes, I care. Haven't I cared all these years? But no doctor comes into this house. I can't afford to have people prying and asking questions."

"Would you let her die?"

"She'll get better."

"Not without help."

Mary put out her hand, groping. "Peter, I can't see you."

"I'm here."

"Where?"

Peter grasped the searching hand and held it.

"Don't leave me!"

"I never have, have I? I'm not likely to do so now."

"My head! Peter, I'm blind."

"No, you're not. When the pain goes you'll be able to see."

But Mary appeared not to hear. She screamed once, raising herself from the pillows, then dropped back and the sound became a whimper, more like that of an injured animal than of a human.

"If you won't go for the doctor, I shall," Marie said, fiercely, and turned and made for the door.

Peter leaped from the bed and caught Marie by the shoulders.

"You'll do as you're told, you half-witted booby! I say you don't leave this house."

"You can't stop me."

"Can't I?"

Peter hit her across the head, a blow which sent her sprawling to the ground. For a few moments she was dazed, and when she could drag herself to her feet she saw that Peter was huddling into a shirt and trousers.

"Now," said Peter, fully clothed, "we'll settle you, my lady." She clutched Marie by the arm and marched her from the room.

"Where are we going?"

"Where you'll give me no more trouble."

"I don't intend to cause trouble."

"Ah, but you would, trouble to me."

Marie struggled, but the hold on her arm only became more painful.

Down the stairs they went, to the door of the cellar, which Peter opened.

"Not there!" Marie cried.

"There you'll be safe, and if you get a thirst—well, there's plenty of good ale."

She gave Marie a push which sent her almost headlong down the stone steps. The heavy door closed, the key turned, the bolt was shot home. Marie was alone in the dark. Carefully she felt her way down the remaining steps. Apart from the door, the cellar had only one means of access, which was a hole in the pavement of the street. Through this the barrels were delivered, being rolled down a temporary ramp afterwards removed. The hole was covered by a pair of stout, oaken trap-doors.

Marie stood looking up. There was a faint line of light where the doors did not quite meet the paving-stones, but even had she been able to open them, they were far above her head, and she had nothing on which to stand. The enormous barrels were immovable on their supports.

She stayed in that spot until she was tired, for even that tiny thread of daylight was a morsel of comfort, but when her legs ached from standing still, she went and sat on the lowest stone step.

How long she would be kept prisoner she did not know. Unless Peter relented, it might well be until the brewers made their next delivery, and when that would be she had no idea. It was difficult to believe that Peter would allow her to starve, but was it not equally difficult to realise that for so long Peter had been a woman in disguise? The reason for the imposture she could not guess, but from Peter's fear of discovery it would seem that her reasons were far from reputable.

Already Marie was thirsty. From a barrel she took a drink, using the small cup that held the overflow. It relieved her, but she shuddered to think that this might be her only means of sustenance. She was also terrified that there might be rats in the cellar. Nothing on earth, she vowed, would persuade her to go to sleep.

The line of light disappeared, and from this she knew that night had come. By now she was ravenously hungry. She took another drink, and to pass the time repeated everything she could remember having been taught and having read. Poems in English, scraps of Latin and French, aloud she recited them, her voice being some sort of company to her and tending to keep her awake.

But the effort made her thirsty. She took another drink, and then another. She was unaccustomed to alcoholic liquor, and her head began to swim. With surprise and a certain feeling of guilt she realised that she was drunk. The sensation was not altogether unpleasant, for she found she was no longer afraid. Carefully, with a feeling almost of flying, she staggered across the cellar, lay down, using the bottom step as a pillow, and fell into a deep drunken sleep.

FOUR

In the morning she woke with a groan. She was stiff and cold from her hard bed, and the smell of the beer produced a sensation of nausea in her stomach. The cause of her pain and discomfort, she realised, must be the drink she had taken, and she wondered at the foolishness of some of Aunt's customers. What benefit to go rolling home, with song and laughter, if they should feel near to dying on the following morning?

She walked up and down, clapping her hands and arms together, to engender some warmth. There was a streak of light around the trap-door. Was that all of light she was ever to see? Would Peter leave her here until she died of starvation? Oh, no! Peter might be merciless, but there was Aunt to be considered. When the pain subsided, Aunt would ask questions, would demand to know where her niece had gone. Surely in a busy ale-house, in a crowded part of London, it was not possible for a girl to vanish without trace! If she shouted, if she thumped upon the door, wouldn't someone hear?

She went to the top of the steps. Her fists made little sound on the solid door. Carefully she searched around the floor of the cellar, by feeling rather than sight, and at last came upon a short iron bar. With this she was able to create a tolerable disturbance, but as there was no result she came to the conclusion that it was too early in the day for customers to have arrived.

Giving up for the time being, she stood under the pavement entrance and called. The dense walls of this underground hole seemed to swallow up her voice, but for a while she continued undaunted. Some people must hear, must be curious that a voice should cry out from beneath their feet. But she had not allowed for the noise of the city, for the horses and the variety of vehicles they drew, for the thousands of conversations which rose like the hum of a vast beehive, and for the fact that, even had she been heard, the sound would have been attributed to no more than a new way of crying new wares.

She stopped, exhausted, and returned to her seat on the step, and had scarcely done so when the door was opened a little way and something was pushed through it. She started up the steps, stumbling, with a wordless cry, intent only upon reaching that light, shining opening. But when it was no more than a foot or two from her outstretched arms it was blotted out as the door bumped shut.

She groped for the object which had been pushed, and it was a plate holding a lump of dry bread. Thankfully she ate the frugal meal. She longed for a drink of water, but had to make do with beer, though she took only sufficient to moisten her lips.

The day seemed to drag interminably, and she was relieved when at last the line of light vanished from above her head and she was provided with another portion of dry bread.

The next morning was the beginning of the third day. This time she waited at the top of the steps, and when the door was opened she pushed with all her strength. It was hopeless. The door was banged with such violence that she was knocked off her feet, and the plate shot over the edge of the steps, breaking as it fell.

Sobbing, she hammered on the door. "Peter! Peter! Please let me out! I'll do anything you want. Please, Peter!"

There was only silence. Still whimpering, she crept down the steps and felt about her carefully until she had found the bread. Still she shouted from time to time, still she beat upon the door, but with little expectation of result. Hope now was running low. Was it not obvious that Peter intended to keep her here for ever? Frightened, lonely, ill-fed, exhausted, she was in that darkness becoming wrapped in a lethargy in which it was too much effort to think or to speculate as to what might happen to her.

On the fourth morning the door was flung wide and Peter stood at the top of the steps. "Come up!" she commanded, abruptly.

Falteringly Marie climbed and stood blinking in the light which hurt her eyes. To her the house seemed strangely silent, and she supposed, vaguely, that it was too early for customers. This reminded her of her fruitless calling and knocking. "Nobody came," she said. "Nobody came at all."

"Of course they didn't! We was closed."

"Why?"

"Out of respect."

The remark did not make sense to Marie. "I want to see Aunt."

"Well, that you can't do."

"Yes, I can, and you shan't stop me."

As soon as the words were out of her mouth she saw that they had been rash and foolish. How could she dare to defy a large, strong woman like Peter, who could easily take her and thrust her back into the cellar? Nervously she looked over her shoulder. The door was still open.

But Peter laughed, almost genially. "You'd have a long way to go, to see Mary, though there's many short cuts."

"What do you mean?"

"She's dead and buried. That's why I shut the house. It's the proper thing to do. Shows respect."

"You let her die? Oh, you're a murderer! I'll tell them about you. I'll see that you get hanged."

"Well, you've got some spirit, I'll say that for you. Ain't you scared o' me? Ain't you feared of what I'll do?"

As realisation dawned, Marie's anger gave place to grief. She burst into tears.

"How could you have been so cruel?"

Peter looked surprised. " 'Twasn't my fault. When she

died I had to report it, and they fetched a doctor. He said he couldn't have done nothing for her. She'd something growing on her brain."

"You wouldn't help her," Marie insisted. "You let her die. You were afraid to have anyone to see her. You've got a secret you're ashamed of."

"I may have a secret, but I ain't ashamed. Lots of people have secrets."

"Like pretending to be a man. Like pretending to be Aunt's husband."

"You shut up!"

Suddenly Marie thought she understood. "That's why you locked me in the cellar. You were afraid I might give you away."

Peter only smiled. "Come on, my lady! I'll show you to your room."

Somewhat reassured, and thankful to leave the cellar behind her, she preceded Peter up the stairs.

Her little bedroom looked much as usual, though she felt she had been away from it for a long time. There was her simple bed, scarcely raised from the floor, and beside it stood an old wooden chest containing her few personal belongings, on top of which were several books Mr Cooperthwayte had lent her. After the cellar it was a friendly refuge, a slice of luxury; and then she saw that something was different. The window had been fitted with iron bars from top to bottom, set closely together. Slowly she went across to it. There was barely room to thrust her hand between the bars, and even if there had been, it would have been of no use, for the frame had been nailed up in such a way that the window was impossible to open.

"Why did you do this?" she demanded.

Peter shrugged her shoulders. "Don't want you running away."

"Why not? Why should you keep me here now that Aunt is—is dead?"

"Well, I reckon the place belongs to you, don't it? 'Tis yours by law, and what would you do with it?"

Marie frowned. This was a puzzling question, and one she had never considered before. Why should she, when the possibility of owning property had been so remote? And what a poor place it was! Dirty, crooked, tumble-down, almost sinking into the mud which seeped from the river to beneath the foundations.

"I've no use for an ale-house," she said. "I shall sell it and—"

"And what?"

She did not know.

Peter saw she was defeated. "From now on I'm the one that tells you what to do, and you'll learn to behave, if you know what's good for you."

Relief changed to alarm. "You're not going to lock me in?"

"That's just what I am a-going to do."

"The window won't open. There's no air. I shall die."

Peter leered, and Marie became aware of the ugliness of this woman, an ugliness that went deep down below mere face and form. "I've allowed for that." She moved aside, and Marie saw that a small hole had been cut in the door. By some bitter irony the carpenter had fashioned it in the shape of a heart. "You'll not suffocate. Now that Mary's gone you're my little nest-egg. You're going to bring me a nice little fortune before I've finished with you."

"I don't know what you mean."

"Maybe not. But you will. I'm free at last. Or almost free."

"You wanted Aunt to die," Marie cried.

"No, I didn't." Peter's expression changed, softened with some emotion Marie did not understand. "I didn't want nothing to happen to her. She was good to me, but she was a fool. She always was a fool."

On an impulse Marie attempted to take advantage of the woman's altered mood. "You can trust me, Peter. Don't shut me in here. I won't give you away."

It was useless. Peter stiffened, grew tense with suspicion. "What's there to give away, eh? What have I done?"

"Nothing. I mean, I don't know anything."

"What did your aunt tell you?" She took two strides and caught the girl's arm, twisting it until Marie cried out with pain.

"She didn't talk about you. Not ever. I thought you were a man."

"That's what you've got to go on thinking," Peter said, fiercely. "If they knew—" She gave the arm an extra vicious wrench, and then let it go. "And what did Mary say about you and your mother?"

Marie was sobbing. "Only my name. She never told me anything but my name."

Peter moved to the door and opened it. "You stay and keep quiet and you'll get into no trouble."

"How long for? How long are you going to keep me prisoner?"

"That depends."

Involuntarily Marie's eyes strayed to the window, which Peter saw. "If you think to be breaking the glass, or calling out, then you'd better think twice. You'll get no help from those outside. You know how it is around here. People don't interfere. They mind their own affairs. So don't draw attention to yourself."

"I won't," Marie agreed, wearily.

Peter smiled. "If you did anything violent I'd have to tell them you were mad. They'd believe me. They know your aunt had a maggot in her brain. Like aunt, like niece, they'd say." Peter went out and shut the door. Marie heard the key turning in the lock. Then Peter spoke again. Marie could see her lips in the heart-shaped aperture. "After all," said Peter, "this is better than Bedlam."

FIVE

The monotony of the days stretching into weeks filled Marie with despair. She watched the people passing to and fro and found herself envying the meanest beggar, the most tarnished woman of the streets. They at least had an illusion of freedom.

To study her few books passed the time and provided for her a semblance of useful purpose, but she was young and healthy, needing physical activity. She invented games to exercise her body, performed acrobatics, danced and sang, but still found herself sinking into a state of hopelessness.

Once, in a moment of despair, she began to scream at the top of her voice. Another time she hammered on the floor. But these revolts were not repeated. Peter came armed with a stick, and tore her clothes from her and beat her upon the back and the buttocks until she begged for mercy.

Yet though Peter seemed sadistic to the point of madness, she evidently did not wish her prisoner to die, for the food she provided was plentiful, if plain, and every week she would carry up a ewer of hot water and say, "There you are! Now wash yourself. Take off your clothes, mind you! All of 'em."

Marie never ceased to be surprised when Peter displayed any sign of ordinary humanity, but most surprised was she, most shocked, at a change which occurred after she had been confined for—how long? She had no idea.

It happened one night as she lay in bed, half asleep, hearing the voices of the last customers as they were turned out and the tavern locked and bolted. The door of her room opened and Peter stood looking in, a candle in her hand.

"You awake?" Peter asked.

Marie sat up, rubbing her eyes. "What's wrong?"

"Nothing. Come with me."

Mystified, still dazed, Marie got out of bed. To be allowed to leave that room was an adventure in which she could scarcely believe.

Peter led the way to the room she had shared with Mary Hay. She set the candle upon a shelf, and motioned to Marie to take a seat upon the bed.

"I miss her," she said, abruptly.

From her slurred speech it was obvious that she had been drinking. Marie was surprised. When Aunt was alive Peter had never been seen to touch strong liquor.

"I was a ticket-of-leave woman," Peter went on. "It was only petty larceny, and when I was free I went to the Discharged Female Prisoners Aid and they got me a situation as a servant."

With part of her mind Marie was listening, but with the other part she was planning to escape. Peter would never make a confession such as this unless she were drunk. In the morning, when she was sober, she would regret it, and what would happen then?

"There's hundreds of criminals working that way. The employers know, but they don't care. They gets 'em cheap and they gets 'em willing. After all, who wants to go back to jail?"

Marie shivered. She was wearing only her nightgown. Now she wondered how she would manage to return to her room and dress and bundle up her few possessions.

"Some of them finds places in fashionable families, but I was put with a small shopkeeper and his wife in Wentworth Street. She was a mean bitch, if ever there was one. She was always on to me, finding fault. I lost my temper in the end, and I killed her."

Marie stared. "You did what?"

"Well, it was accidental. I knocked her down. How was I to know she'd hit her head on that steel fender, which was as sharp as a sword? Of course I had to get away quickly else it'd have been the gallows for me for sure. So I came here."

Peter fell silent, and Marie began to fear she had finished. What now? Still having no plan, Marie asked, to gain time, "Did you tell Aunt what had happened?"

"Ay, and she was willing to help. She sort of took a fancy to me, and she dressed me as a man, and we concocted the story that I was her husband come back from sea. That way nobody would suspect. She was good to me, was Mary Hay."

Peter looked as though she might be about to cry, but Marie prayed she would fall asleep.

"You must be tired," she said softly, and stood up.

With a violent movement Peter turned and thrust her down on to the bed, on to her back. "You stay where you are. You stay here for to-night."

"I want to go back to my own room."

"You stay here," Peter insisted. " 'Tis melancholy, being alone. I'll let you stay. I'll be good to you if you'll be good to me." She put out her hand, fastened it greedily round one of Marie's scarcely mature breasts. "You're so young, young and sweet. Sweet enough to eat." She released her hold, and ran her hand down Marie's body, on top of the nightgown, pressing into every valley, every crevice.

Marie lay rigid. She was more terrified than she could remember ever having been. No beating she had received had been as bad as this.

With a sudden swift movement she twisted from that exploring hand, made a lunge for the door. But before she was through it Peter had caught hold of her, pulled her away, then locked the door and taken out the key. "I'll put this on a string around my neck," she said, "in case you feel like taking a walk while I'm asleep. Now you come and lie down."

"I won't!"

Peter lifted her and flung her on to the bed. "You'll do what I tell you. You're my little sweetheart, ain't you?" She laid herself down beside Marie, almost on top of her, and her arm was heavy across Marie's body. "I ain't a-going to hurt you, only cuddle you."

Marie closed her eyes. She would try to forget the woman was there, and after a few minutes, to her relief, Peter fell asleep, but Marie lay awake for a considerable time, wondering what was best to do. If she further antagonised Peter, she would gain nothing except closer restraint. If, on the other hand, she humoured her, might she not find an opportunity for escaping?

So, hoping and praying she might have sufficient strength of will, she set about cultivating a friendship with the ex-convict, talking to her, professing an interest in her past life of crime.

Peter was suspicious, veering between sullen mistrust and cringing solicitude. She found herself in effect the landlord of a tavern. With the money she could do as she pleased, though that was no fortune. Recently trade had fallen off, for strange tales were going about. Some said Mary had not died naturally. And what had happened to that niece of hers? The blind reader and writer, the Reverend Cooperthwayte, had gone round to the Leather Bottle to see his pupil, and had been told she was away to the country.

If Peter heard the rumours, she took no notice of them. So long as the barrels were full, she had free drink, and so long as she took enough money to replace the empty barrels, she was satisfied, or nearly satisfied. To make easy money had been her life's ambition, if ambition it could be called, and now, freed from Mary's control, she saw the way to do so. Fuddled with drink she might be, but she still had a certain criminal cunning which was quicker to see an illegal opening than a lawful one, and when she called Marie her little nest-egg, she meant what she said.

Every night after that first one, Marie was taken to Peter's bed. In the beginning the prospect coloured her whole day with dread, but Peter was now drinking so heavily that she usually fell into a deep sleep immediately upon lying down, and Marie was not troubled by her unwelcome caresses.

After a time Marie conjured up sufficient courage to make a suggestion. "Can't I come down to the bar and help you serve drinks?"

"Take me for a simpleton?" Peter sneered. "You'd be off faster than a streak o' lightning. 'Sides, you ain't old enough."

"I'll soon be seventeen. Leastways, I reckon so from what Aunt told me."

"What else did your aunt tell you?"

"What sort of thing do you mean?"

"About your mother."

"Her name was Jane, and she lived in France."

"I know that," Peter said, impatiently. "I just wondered whether Mary let slip anything else."

"She wouldn't tell me if she didn't tell you. Oh, Peter, please let me out of here!"

"Girl, you must think I'm crazed. I've got other plans besides finishing my life at the end of a rope. You're my only danger."

"I wouldn't betray you."

"You'll not get the chance. Maybe I'm soft. Maybe I should have rid myself of you months ago, left you in the cellar."

"That would be murder."

"What difference, one murder or two? I can only hang once."

Marie looked down, to hide the fear she knew she was showing. Was it all wasted, her attempt to gain Peter's confidence, her simulated friendliness? Was her life really at risk?

"We can't go on for ever in this way," she said, dejectedly.

Peter got up. "No," she replied, briskly, "we can't. I've been expecting to hear something, but if there's no news soon I'll have to give up the plan." She looked at Marie, and there was a strange sadness in her face. "Soft I may be, but not soft enough to kiss the gallows for the sake of a dainty body and a head of red hair."

SIX

Hour upon hour Marie would sit attempting to devise some means of escape from her prison, and when, as always, she failed to do so she would turn to puzzling over Peter's vague but terrifying threats. What could be the news Peter was expecting? What the plan she might be compelled to give up? Had Aunt let drop to her pretended husband some clues of which her niece was ignorant? Frustrated and bewildered, Marie would pace the length of her small room until from cramped weariness she was forced to rest again.

At night she was still taken to Peter's bed, though the reason for this seemed obscure, since Peter slept heavily the whole of the time. Perhaps it was because of a deep-seated loneliness in Peter, a grieving for Mary, a need to have someone beside her while she slept and when dazed and confused she awoke. This period was the only one during which Marie could hope to escape, and once or twice she had made tentative efforts to remove the key from Peter's neck, but even in sleep Peter seemed on guard, and her hand would close about the key protectively.

Drunk or sober, Peter was a cunning woman, one who had lived by what wits she had, crafty though not clever. To hoodwink her was, Marie came to the conclusion, beyond her powers. Yet, since she had nothing better to do, she found herself going round and round the problem, and always she came back to the one thing which might have helped her—her mother's letter, the missing letter.

What was it Aunt had said?" "I can't give you the letter

because I haven't got it. I kept it safe, as I thought, but it disappeared."

How could such a letter get lost, the last letter from a sister? Who would throw it away? And all the time Mary and Peter and the child had been in the same place. The letter had lain in the Leather Bottle, in the private quarters into which customers never strayed. To find it might be to have the answers to some of the questions which buzzed like hornets about her head.

Mary Hay had never made sufficient money to indulge in luxuries, and the Leather Bottle was not an inn, catering for travellers, so the upstairs chambers were more than half empty. Only in Mary's room, with its bed, closet, chest of drawers and coffer, was the letter likely to be secreted.

At this realisation Marie was so excited that she could scarcely wait until night. She counted herself stupid for not having thought of it before, and yet an earlier attempt might well have ended in failure, for only now could Peter be relied upon to sleep heavily enough to give Marie time and opportunity to search.

It went as she hoped. Peter sank into a drunken stupor, and Marie had only to decide whether it were better to light the candle and look immediately for the letter, or to wait until morning and seek in daylight. To be found investigating by candlelight would be to put an end for ever to her hope of obtaining the letter, yet was not this the hour when Peter would be sleeping most heavily?

She decided to risk it. The single candle, which ordinarily seemed so dull, burned with what appeared to be a dangerously brilliant light. With her hand she shielded it and glanced towards the bed. Peter was lying on her back, snoring. Was she really in such a deep sleep? Marie moved towards the chest of drawers. A board cracked like a shot from a gun. Peter snorted and the snoring ceased. Marie could not look at her. She froze into the stillness of a statue. There was a rustling as Peter turned on to her side.

Marie waited, not daring to put another foot forward. The

candlestick trembled with her fear and chilliness, and a spot of hot tallow fell on to her hand. How long she stood thus she did not know, but as the silence continued unbroken she took courage, and feeling the floor with each foot before putting her weight on it, she took three more paces.

There were five drawers to be searched, two short ones at the top and three long ones. She put the candle on the floor, and the consequent dimming of its light gave her a sense of protection.

The two small drawers ran easily enough, but the long ones jammed and creaked, and as she struggled with them she could not believe Peter would not wake. Only a kind of obstinacy and the boldness of despair helped her to continue, and when she had finished she sat on the floor, breathless and despondent. She refused to admit the absence of the letter. Had she not been thorough in her examination of the drawers? Should she go through them again? The letter must be there. Ah, but she was weary, and she knew she could not face once more the pulling and the pushing, the sudden noises she could not avoid.

There remained only the coffer, but who would place a letter in a chest which had no shelves, no nooks and corners? Almost she gave up, but if she did not finish the business this time, she was sure she would not be able to undertake it again.

The lid of the coffer was heavy, but at least it opened soundlessly, and there, neatly folded, lay Mary Hay's clothes.

The garments were plain and few. One by one Marie removed them, opening them and feeling for any crackle of paper. She did it to satisfy herself that the letter was not here, rather than from any hope of success, and as she handled the well-worn clothes she thought of Mary Hay. Poor Aunt! To come into the world and then depart, leaving only a dimming memory in the minds of one or two, a poor grave with no headstone, and a few articles of clothing to provide a meal for the moths.

Here was her best dress, in violet crape, with a narrow

edging of lace at the throat and wrists. With a gesture of regret, of affection, Marie laid her hand on it and felt what was there, and knew, without a moment's doubt, that this was the letter, carefully tucked up the sleeve.

Now that she had found it, she was calm. She put back the clothes and shut the lid of the coffer, wondering why she was not in a panic, for this was the time of greatest danger, when Peter might discover she had the letter. There was nowhere in her loose nightgown where she might hide it, so she returned to bed, placed it under her pillow, and blew out the light.

Morning was the time when Peter was in her worst temper. She felt queasy and cantankerous and out of sorts and resentful. Life was unfair to her, she held, and it certainly was not her fault. It was the fault of whoever happened to be around, and lately this had been Marie.

She dragged on some clothes, and then unlocked the door. "Come on!" she ordered "Stir your lazy bones. D'you expect to lie in bed all day?"

Such a question was unreasonable, since Marie was permitted no occupation, but on this particular morning she was indeed reluctant to leave her bed. She slid her hand under the pillow. There was the precious letter, but could she manage to smuggle it out without discovery? Peter was standing there, watching her.

She sat up in bed. "Oh!"

"Come along! No malingering, or by the holy poker and the tumbling Tom I'll warm your backside." This was an oath Peter had learned from some of her Irish customers.

"No, I heard something, truly I did. There's someone trying the door."

"If they think they can come bothering me at crack o'dawn—"

In a few strides Peter was across the room, looking out of the window. It did not take long, but it was sufficient time for Marie to stuff the folded letter up her sleeve. If she kept her hands together, her arm horizontal, it would be safe.

"Nobody there!" Peter exclaimed. "Are you having me on?"

Without a word Marie went to her own room, Peter following. For the first time there was a great relief in hearing the key turn in the lock.

The very feeling of the letter in her hands was a comfort and a caress, for it was as though it were the end of a line joining her to her mother, to the father who was not even a name and to all the unknown members of her family. The letter eased the pain of the loneliness and fear of the past few months. Not immediately did she feel the necessity of reading it. It was sufficient to hold it.

But presently natural curiosity returned. She sprang from her bed and went to the window, to obtain the best light for the seventeen-year-old writing. Her hands were so shaking with excitement that the paper rustled like autumn leaves.

"My Dearest Sister,

Though we have been estranged, I write to ask of you a favour, and to beg your forgiveness for the grief I must have caused you."

Marie stopped. Her eyes were blinded with tears, for it was as though her mother had come to life.

She took out her handkerchief, wiped her eyes, and continued. "Alone in the world as we were, I should have stayed with you. But, as you know, I was always a lover of beautiful and luxurious things, and to live in a house such as Rippiers, even as a servant, was a temptation I could not resist.

"Of course I had to accompany the family when they returned to France. I loved Rodolphe so much, and he loved me. Yes, Mary, it was love not lechery which made him take me, and we were married secretly in Paris. But he did not dare to tell his family. Already they were planning an advantageous marriage for him. Oh, not with one of the remaining nobility! Such ideas are extremely passé nowadays. This was to be a political match, with the daughter of a person in power. But before it could be arranged, Rodolphe took a fever. I think he was in a low state of health, being hard pressed by his family.

"Oh, Mary, how shall I live without him? Before he died, he confessed to our marriage, and they were all very angry with me, but he insisted that he should see me, and so I was with him at the end.

"He tried to smile, and said, 'Poor Jane! They'll not treat you well, but remember the treasure. You are entitled to that.'

"It was something we had talked about, a kind of family legend, but I'd not taken it seriously, and I was not interested. My heart was breaking because Rodolphe was dying.

"His breathing changed then, and he could scarcely speak, but he beckoned me closer and whispered something which sounded like 'Forty footsteps.'

"He was right about the family not treating me well. Rodolphe's brother Gustave and Gustave's wife would not allow me to attend the funeral, and the Marquis—no, that was what we called him, from courtesy. Officially he was known as Citizen Vaudelet, not even 'de Vaudelet.' Anyway, he commanded me to leave the house. I was glad to do so, because had I stayed longer they would have discovered I was with child, and I was afraid of what they might do to me.

"So I came to Paris, and a month ago my little daughter was born. Mary, there has been another revolution, and I am sorely afraid. How far it will go I cannot tell, but armed men came to search my room two days ago, and I hear Louis-Philippe is on his way to England, if he has not already landed. They are making barricades in the streets, and I have heard the sound of firing.

"I must have my baby taken to safety. As yet I am too weak to move, but there is a Frenchman I can trust. He needs to flee the country, and as Rodolphe was his friend he is willing to take my child with him.

"She has been christened, and I have called her after you, but in the French fashion. Her full name is Marie Annette

Madeleine Veronique. When I am strong enough I will follow, but should anything happen to me, oh, Mary, care for her as if she were your own. In God's name do this, and for the peace of mind of your loving and persecuted sister.
Jane."

SEVEN

Not once did Marie read this letter, but many times. She read it until she knew it by heart, so that if Peter should discover and confiscate it, it would be with her always, in her mind. As she learned the words, she sought the meaning beneath them and the nature of the writer. Her mother must have been a gentle woman, yet gay and brave and passionate as well. In a titled gentleman she had inspired love, not lust, and when he died she had had the courage to slip away to revolution-racked Paris for the sake of her unborn child.

Though the next few days passed slowly enough, they were in some subtle manner less tedious than all those which had gone before. Vanished was that feeling of being lost and alone, of belonging nowhere. Marie had a name and a family, one of which she need never be ashamed. Around her stood her ancestors, ghostly but comforting, and to them she could give whatever faces and attributes her imagination contrived.

She was so cheerful that Peter noticed the difference and cast suspicious glances at her. "What have you got to be so jaunty about, my lady?"

"I don't know. It must be the spring."

"And how would you know the time of year?"

"Why, easily. The mornings are light, and the sparrows chirp so loudly they almost drown the grinding of the cart-wheels."

Peter sniffed. "That's not enough to put such a smirk upon your face. Are you keeping something from me?"

"Don't be silly! How could I keep secrets from you?"

"Don't you tell me not to be silly!" Peter put her hand across Marie's face, pressing on her cheeks until the tears came to her eyes. "I'm getting tired of you, and I'm getting tired of this miserable ale-house. I never was one for enjoying work." She released Marie and walked to the window. "It don't look as if what I planned is coming to pass. I'll give it another week, and then I'll set about selling this place."

"You can't. It doesn't belong to you."

"It will. You'll write a paper saying as you makes it over to me."

"I will not!" Marie declared, boldly. "You can't make me do it."

"Can't I?" She walked towards the door, smiling, and Marie thought Peter's smile was one of the most mirthless things she had seen, and one of the most frightening. "Can't I? Reckon I'm pretty good at persuading people to do things, even if they're not particularly wishful to do 'em."

Marie's light-heartedness evaporated, and she became even more alarmed when that evening Peter neither fetched her to share her bed nor brought supper for her. What now lay in store for her? Was starvation to be her fate?

But on the following morning there was food, though Peter did not address one word to her. Perhaps, Marie thought, hopefully, it was just a passing fit of bad temper on Peter's part, and, her fears allayed, she turned her thoughts once more to her mother and father. It pleased and amused her to reflect on her name, which in full would be Marie Annette Madeleine Veronique de Vaudelet. But that sounded pretentious for an ordinary girl like herself. Better be plain Marie Vaudelet, and be thankful she had a legal right to a fine old name.

So bemused was she with what she had learned about her family that she was foolish enough to write down her name on the fly-leaf of one of her books and to leave the cover open.

Peter saw it. She said nothing, but went out immediately, and from the banging and thumping which followed, Marie guessed that a search for the letter was in progress.

When Peter returned she was in a fine rage. "Now you've cooked your goose, you bounceful little baggage! Steal from me, would you!"

"What are you talking about?"

"The letter."

"If you mean the letter my mother wrote to my aunt, you've no right to it."

Peter did not reply, but tore the covers from the bed, and dragged away the thin mattress, and picked up Marie's books, shaking them and tearing the covers from them, and strewed the floor with Marie's clothes, pulling them apart where she could, and ripping off the sleeves.

Helplessly Marie watched this work of destruction until at last, breathless, Peter stopped. "All right! So you've got it on you."

She grabbed the girl, shaking her until Marie was dizzy, then plunged her large, rough hand down the front of Marie's dress, to where the letter nestled between her breasts. It was not enough for Peter to take the letter; she pinched and squeezed until Marie cried out with pain, and still the punishment went on, until at last she stopped and went out, leaving Marie, half fainting, lying among the ruin of her few possessions.

That was when Marie came closest to despair. She thought, there is nothing for me, no hope, no future. Half-heartedly she set about putting the room to some semblance of order. Most of her garments were unwearable. The worn ticking of the mattress had split under Peter's assault, and the sharp spikes of straw protruded, refusing to lie flat. As for the books, Marie wept when she looked at them.

She lay down on the miserable bed, her body bruised and aching, and wished she had never been born. What purpose could there be in a life like hers?

Days passed as she remained in this wretched state, and then one morning, when the sun shone so brightly that it filled the room with a golden light, Peter unlocked the door and announced, "You've got a visitor," and added, over her shoulder to someone behind her, "This is her."

"I would wish to see her alone," said a man's voice.

"Please yourself!" Peter sounded surly. "But I'll have to lock the door."

"Surely it is not necessary—"

"Leave her loose and she'd be off like a hare. I'll come back pretty soon, don't you worry!"

Slowly, with seeming reluctance, the visitor stepped into the room, and Peter, after securing the door, could be heard stumping down the stairs.

Marie's first sensation was one of shame. She sat up and pulled the bedcovers to her chin. She was unkempt, unwashed, her hair uncombed, and for a few minutes she could not raise her eyes to look at the newcomer.

"That man, is he mad?" he asked.

Suddenly Marie forgot her appearance. She was interested, curious. "He is not a man. He's a woman. You are foreign, aren't you?"

She looked up as she spoke, and he bowed. "French. Alain Vaudelet."

She sprang to her feet. "Vaudelet! You are a Vaudelet! Oh, my goodness! We are related."

He looked round, and she quickly pushed the only chair towards him. "Please sit down! The back is broken, but the seat is quite firm."

He hesitated. "Will you not—"

"I'll sit on the bed."

He was quite a young man, about twenty-five, she guessed, and extremely handsome and elegant. There were certain peculiarities in his dress which marked him as a foreigner, and which in Wapping were almost sufficient to cause him to be mobbed. He wore a crush hat, his coat was exceedingly full in the skirts, and on his feet were shiny black boots. On his upper lip was a pair of dark moustaches trimmed and trained to needle-sharp points. As he seated himself he laid across his knees his light silver-topped cane.

"I understand you to be the daughter of the servant."

Immediately she was hostile. "My mother was the wife of the Marquis de Vaudelet," she stormed. "He married her lawfully, and you are to say nothing against her."

"Have you proof?"

"Yes. It is in her letter which I—no! Peter has it."

"Ah! Well, she was a servant in our household," Alain said calmly. "This you cannot deny. She accompanied us to France. I remember her well, though I was but a small boy at the time."

"You remember her?" Marie's anger dissolved as easily as an April cloud. "You don't know how wonderful it is to meet someone who knew my mother. What was she like, my mother? What was she like?"

"I forget. There is no picture of her in my mind."

So swiftly disappointment swept over her joy and excitement that she started to cry. "You said you remembered her."

"Yes, but one does not notice servants particularly, does one?"

"Rodolphe did."

"My uncle? Yes, he evidently noticed her." Alain spoke drily.

"Your uncle? Then who are you?"

"The son of Gustave, Uncle Rodolphe's brother. I am, I suppose, your cousin."

She stared at him, trying to assimilate this information. That this fashionable gentleman should actually be her cousin! It was incredible.

"Is my mother dead?"

He shrugged his shoulders. "I know as little of this matter as you do, but I think she must be dead. Would she not otherwise have followed you to England?"

"But didn't you-I mean, didn't your father try to find her?"

"Why should he? Do you imagine my family looked with

favour upon such a match? I think he was somewhat harsh in turning her away, but-"

"He did not know about me."

"No, he did not know about you."

There was silence as each of the two was filled with thoughts, similar perhaps, yet perhaps of very different significance.

At last Marie said, "You speak English well."

"I was at school in England, and, after all, I was born in England in our English residence."

"Where is that?"

He hesitated. "Do you not know?"

"I know scarcely anything of my family, only what was in Mother's letter. Has Peter shown you the letter?"

"Peter seems extraordinarily secretive. What is he—she to you?"

"Nothing!" Marie declared, passionately. "She is a former convict, a ticket-of-leave woman. My aunt befriended her."

"I see." Alain regarded her critically. "You speak like an educated young lady."

"I am educated," Marie replied, with pride. "I had a tutor who was a learned man."

"Yet you have the appearance of a beggar or a gipsy."

"What else would you expect?" Marie asked, furiously. "Peter has ill-treated me, laid violent hands on me. How can I look other than I do?"

"I am sorry. I did not intend to insult you."

"But you have come to rescue me, haven't you? You will take me away from here, won't you?"

He did not answer for a moment or two, and then he said, "It could be a plot, something you have concocted between the two of you."

"A plot? What do you mean?"

"How do I know you are whom you claim to be?"

She was at a loss. "But I—I—"

"Have you not wondered how I learned of your existence?"

"Oh, heavens, I wonder so many things that my head is spinning."

"Apparently this woman Peter found the name de Vaudelet in your mother's letter, and guessing it must be a famous name in France she sent out inquiries. It was not difficult here, where there are so many sailors and so much traffic with the Continent. That is how I heard of you."

"You were surprised?"

"Not so much as you might expect. I have a sister, and before our mother died she confessed to her that she knew the servant to be pregnant. She did not tell my father, for fear he would have taken pity on the girl and kept her. Do not look so shocked! My mother acted from a natural maternal instinct."

"And you have come to make amends," Marie said, happily, as though she were reading an old romance where everything must be right at the finish.

"Officially the title has ceased to exist," Alain told her. "We are all citizens now."

Marie ignored this. What were titles, anyway? "Even Peter must have some spark of conscience, or she would not have searched for you."

Alain stood up. He looked grim. "Peter's motive is on a level with all her other transactions. Her desire to find me was purely commercial."

"Why? What does she want?"

"She plans," said Alain, "to sell you to me, and for a considerable sum of money."

EIGHT

"Sell me?" Marie imagined that she had not heard aright.
"Sell me? Who would want to—"

She got no further before the door opened and Peter stood
waiting.

Alain nodded to Peter. "I am ready."

"Not yet! Oh, please not so soon!" Marie cried. Scores of
questions were racing through her mind, and she felt a great
fear that if he went he would never return.

"I will return," Alain said. "I will return tomorrow."

She did not know whether to believe him or not. He might
be speaking out of pity. He might even be going to fetch the
police, believing, as he had suggested, that she was in league
with Peter to extort money from him.

Fortunately there were things to be done. "Bring me a
bath and water," she demanded of Peter, "many cans of
water. I wish to wash my body and my head."

"Why, is his lordship afeared of bugs?"

"I don't suppose Monsieur Vaudelet has ever seen a
louse," Marie said, with dignity, "and it's shameful he
should find his cousin in the condition I'm in."

"Oh, la-de-dah! So he's your cousin, is he? Moving in high
society, ain't we? I only hope his bank-roll is as long as his
lovely moustachios."

Marie swung round. "How could you be so stupid as to
demand money from him? Don't you know you could go to
prison for that? And with your record it would most likely
mean the hangman."

Peter contrived to look the picture of injured innocence.

"There's nothing criminal in being paid for an introduction and it's me that brought your long-lost cousin back to you."

"You offered to sell me to him."

"Sell you? I never used such a word. Why should I? Still, he's a foreigner, and you can't expect a foreigner to speak English nice like we do."

Peter turned to go out of the room, but there was one more thing Marie felt she must know. "Did you show him my mother's letter?"

"D'you want me to?"

"Yes, of course! That's the only way I can prove who I am."

"Then I shan't show him. Leastways, not yet." Peter tapped her nose with her finger. "Got to see the colour of his money first."

Marie made the best of herself and of her room. With her clothes there was little she could do, but her freshly-washed hair had the sheen of chestnut kernels, and she left it loose, hanging over her shoulders down to her waist.

She was so torn between hope and fear that she could not keep still, but from dawn on the following morning was moving to the window to look out, and from there to the door, to listen. Close on mid-day Alain arrived. Her doubts about her appearance vanished when he gave her a wondering look, but he said nothing until Peter had departed, again locking the door behind her. Then he moved to the window, beckoning to Marie to stand beside him.

"We must speak quietly. I believe that woman is listening."

"I heard her go downstairs."

"We would not know if she should come back. Marie—" He lifted his hand, a white, well-manicured gentleman's hand, and took up a strand of her hair. "Marie, you are a beautiful young lady."

It was the first time such a compliment had been paid her. She was embarrassed, and could find only one thing to say. "Was my mother beautiful?"

Alain sighed. "Do you think of no-one and nothing but your mother?"

"She's all I have."

"I have told you, I forget how she looked."

"Maybe you forget her features," Marie insisted, "but you'd know if she were beautiful or ugly."

"I was only so high, five or six years old."

Marie nodded, and asked, "Has Peter shown you the letter?"

"No, she refuses to do so until I have paid her the money."

"Then you must, quickly."

Alain stared at her in amazement. "Must?"

"Of course!" Marie spoke impatiently, because to her it seemed perfectly clear what Alain should do. "If you don't, you'll never have proof of my identity, and she'll never set me free. Don't you understand?"

"I understand," he said, slowly, "but I do not agree with you. I cannot allow myself to be the victim of such flagrant trickery. It is a matter of principle." He looked so grave and stern as he said this that Marie was deeply impressed and felt she had displayed a lack of refinement.

"Then what can we do?" she asked.

"Why, we must get you away from here as soon as possible, but without paying ransom to that evil woman."

"It won't be easy."

He smiled. "I do not enjoy to have things too easy. Tell me, Marie, do you know what is in your mother's letter?"

Impulsively she cried, "Yes, yes! I have it word for word."

"So we do not have to depend on Madame Peter," he told her, gaily.

"And you believe I am Marie Vaudelet?"

"Yes, I believe it. I believe you are my charming and beautiful cousin."

His words filled her with such joy that she felt nothing was impossible. "I know! When Peter opens the door, we push her aside and run down the stairs."

Alain looked shocked. "How can I take you with me as your are?"

"I am clean," she told him. "I have washed."

"Dear cousin, you have not looked at yourself. Your gown hangs in tatters from you. Your toes peep through your shoes. You are scarcely decent."

She stared at him in dismay. "How shall we get away then?"

"Why, we shall dress you tolerably. I will instruct the woman to buy boots for you, and arrange for a dressmaker to visit you."

"But that will take days!"

"What of it? We are young, Marie. We have many years ahead of us. Leave it to me."

She didn't believe Peter would agree to Alain's suggestion, but apparently she did, for the very next morning she brought with her a small frail mouse of a woman and announced, "This is the dressmaker."

The woman gazed at the room and at Marie with repugnance, but set about taking her measurements while Peter watched and advised. "Nothing fancy, mind you!" Peter said. "The person what's paying for it wants it done in a couple o' days, so it's the plainer the quicker, if you see what I mean. She'll need only a petticoat, a walking dress and a bonnet."

"The wind is still cold," the dressmaker observed, severely. "She should have a paletot."

Peter shrugged her shoulders. "Please yourself! If you like to sit up all night sewing—"

The woman, on her knees with the measuring tape in her hand, looked up at Marie. "Perhaps a silver-grey alpaca, practical and hard-wearing. And the latest fashion is for short dresses, only to the ankle. Do you think—"

"I think," Peter interrupted, "you'll lose the order if you spend the day gossiping. She ain't going to a court ball, you know."

"I must get the length right," the dressmaker insisted.

"Twaddle!" Peter snorted. "If you're not finished in five minutes I'll throw you down the stairs."

She was finished in two minutes, and scuttled away, convinced she was dealing with bedlamites or rogues, or both. She was half inclined to ignore the commission, but she badly needed the money.

So the work was completed within the two days, delivered, and paid for by Peter.

Peter took the clothes to Marie, together with a pair of boots she had bought. "Here you are! Put these on when you get up. Reckon your high and mighty cousin'll be here in the morning."

Marie looked at her with some curiosity. "Are you really going to set me free?"

"Why not? You're an encumbrance, that's what you are. But before you go, you write me that paper saying as the Leather Bottle belongs to me."

"I've never promised to do any such thing."

"You won't go unless you do it. Well, what d'you want with a crummy place like this?" Peter spoke in an almost wheedling tone. "You've got your wealthy relations now. You'll have more money than you can spend."

"I don't know." Marie was uncertain. "My cousin and I have never discussed money."

"Rich folk don't need to discuss it. They just spends it. Let me bring you a nice new pen, and you can sign now that the tavern's mine."

"No, I can't do it until I've spoken to Alain."

"Have it your own way, miss! But you're not leaving here until it's done."

So the door was locked. Marie hoped it would be the last time such a thing would happen to her, and in the morning she dressed in her new clothes, and sat waiting for Alain. The dressmaker had made a poor job of such a rush order. There was no lace or braiding on the dress or paletot, no flowers or feathers on the bonnet, but no fine lady could have felt finer than Marie did as she perched stiffly on the edge of a chair, fearful of crumpling her skirt or disturbing the set of her bonnet.

NINE

The time of waiting seemed long, but at last she heard footsteps on the stairs, and stood up, carefully smoothing her skirt, and as Alain entered the room she gazed expectantly at him. What she hoped to hear she did not know. Perhaps an expression of surprise or approval. But he did not mention her appearance, merely said, "Ah, so you are ready."

She picked up a small parcel she had made, a couple of books less mutilated than the rest, and odds and ends accumulated by one who had few possessions.

"I have a cab waiting," Alain told her.

He stood back to allow Marie to precede him, but Peter was blocking the doorway.

"No, you don't!" Peter exclaimed. "None of that! I'll have my money before you leave this room."

Marie held her breath. Now surely Alain would need to resort to force. What he would do she had no idea. Frenchmen, she understood, were particularly inclined to chivalry.

But Alain did nothing sensational. He merely laughed and took from beneath his travelling cloak a leather bag.

"Here is your remuneration, and you are an extortioner, but it seems I have no choice except to pay."

Peter grabbed the bag and began fumbling with the drawstring, which was twice knotted at the top, but Alain put his hand over it. "No, we cannot wait while you count your booty. We have to take the railway-train to Brighton, and there is little time. But shake the bag. Feel the weight of it. It is filled with golden guineas."

As he was speaking he pushed Marie before him, and

hurried her down the stairs and out of the door, and ran with her along the alley to where the cab waited in the High Street. As they started off he glanced over his shoulder and she thought he seemed apprehensive.

"Are you afraid of Peter?" she asked.

"One must always be cautious of such rogues."

"You said you would not give her the money."

"Yes, but how else could I effect your escape?"

She wanted to express her gratitude, but was still shy, and could only smile at him. "Peter said she would not let me go until I had signed a paper giving her the tavern."

"I think Peter was overwhelmed by the large bag of money, and confused by our swift departure."

"So we shall never see her again."

"I hope we shall not."

"And we are truly to travel on a railway-train to Brighton?"

"Truly."

She tried to hide her excitement. He would think her a foolish child, and so she determined to act like a woman of the world. There should be no exclamations of amazement, no pointing to objects of wonder.

But the sight of the sea, so vast, and of the people braving this monster by paddling at the edge, or even taking a dip further out, was more than her resolution could endure. She clapped her hands and jumped like a child.

Alain pointed to the crowded beach. "They call this the 'London ordinary', because people come for eight hours at the seaside and dine here, in the open air."

"It must be pleasant," Marie replied. "Can we not do the same?"

Alain looked shocked. "With that mob? My dear girl, we might contract the most loathsome diseases."

"They look a good deal cleaner than most of the people in Wapping."

"Which is no standard from which to judge. We shall dine

in more civilised fashion, and I think it high time we went to book our rooms."

They stayed that night at the Bristol Hotel, and Marie was puzzled by the break in their journey.

"I thought we were going to your country house."

"So we are."

"Then why are we staying here?"

"Because we still have about fifty miles more to travel."

"It is a long distance from London."

"Ah, but we have not taken the direct route. Brighton is not on our road."

"Well, why did we come?"

Alain glanced sideways at her. For a moment he seemed at a loss, and then he said, "I brought you that I might show you what is considered to be the foremost marine town in Europe. Besides—well, we do not wish everyone to know where we are going, do we?"

"You mean Peter? She won't trouble us, now that she has the money. Are we to travel on another railway train?"

"No, I shall hire a carriage, and we shall set off in the morning and lie up one more night, perhaps in Battle."

Marie did not speak for a few minutes, and Alain smiled at her. "You are lost in a dream."

"I was thinking— What is it like, Rippiers?"

"Rippiers!" He looked surprised. "How do you come to know the name of the house?"

"Mother mentioned it in her letter."

"Did she say where it was situated?"

"No. Just the name."

"Ah!" Strangely, he seemed relieved.

"Has it to be a secret?" Marie asked. "You are afraid of Peter, aren't you?"

"Why should I fear such a creature?"

"Well, you gave her a lot of money, after you said you wouldn't do it. You made us run quickly to get away from her. You did not wait for Mother's letter."

"Had I waited—" He broke off. "No matter! You remember the contents."

"I don't know—I don't know that I shall always remember." Already, it seemed, her mother's words were becoming hazy. With so many new sights, the picture of those two precious sheets of paper was wavering; with so many new sounds, the voice she imagined as her mother's was fading.

"Then you must write it all down." Alain commanded. "As soon as we arrive at Rippiers."

The next morning they set off at a spanking pace, the horses' coats gleaming in the sun, and the newly-painted carriage positively sparkling. The railway train had been fascinating, even awesome, but this, on such a lovely day, was the best way to travel.

Yet Alain apparently did not find it so pleasureable, for as they left Brighton on the road for Lewes he kept looking round. There was a considerable amount of traffic at first, and it was not until they were in the country and were the only vehicle in sight that he took a deep breath and sat back, more at ease.

From Lewes they took an easterly direction, skirting the town of Hailsham and the villages of Hellingly and Hurstmonceaux. To Marie, accustomed to the thickly populated districts of London, the landscape had a look of wildness and emptiness. So many green fields there were, so many mysterious woodlands. If the carriage should founder in a ditch, she thought, and they should be injured, would anyone ever find them, or would they lie, like the babes in the wood, until the birds and the winds of next autumn covered them with leaves?

This idea so frightened her that she moved closer to Alain, needing the touch of him for security.

He looked startled. "Have you not sufficent room?"

"Yes, thank you." She eased herself away. "I slipped."

He smiled. "Not surprising. They have polished the leather almost too thoroughly."

At Ninfield he stopped the carriage, to point out the vista

of the English Channel, with Pevensey Bay and the coast-towns of Hastings and Eastbourne. It was all laid out so peacefully. No longer did she have the impression of being in a wilderness, and only five miles ahead was the busy market town of Battle.

Yet Marie was slightly troubled. The horses and the carriage still shone brightly, but a little of the polish had been rubbed from her enjoyment. Alain had not wanted her close to him. He had been uncomfortable and resentful of her touch.

PART TWO

Rippiers

ONE

After they left Battle, themselves and the horses refreshed by the night's rest, they drove along country lanes, through a region of woods and hills, and though they came upon villages, as well as scattered farmhouses, Marie was again aware of the sensation that they were leaving the world of people and entering a wilderness where the true inhabitants were animals and birds and trees. She felt like a trespasser, one who might walk into a trap, disappear, be swallowed by the soft, spongy greenness.

Not again did she attempt to seek comfort by moving closer to Alain, since he appeared to find her proximity distasteful, but she was sure the sound of his voice would dispel her foolish fancies, and she did not believe he could object to a little conversation.

"How much further have we to go?" she asked.

"It is sixteen miles from Battle to Rye, and we have travelled about nine, I should imagine.

"There are scarcely any people."

This amused him. "Would you expect to find crowds congregating?"

"The villages have pretty names. Sedlescombe, Brede, Udimore."

"My favourite is Udimore," Alain told her, "for it comes from a French name—eau de mer, water of the sea. Once the sea came right up to it, but now the fickle ocean has deserted Rye."

"What of our house, what of Rippiers?"

He looked at her curiously. "*Our* house?"

"Well, we are cousins, are we not? Therefore the house must belong to both of us."

He hesitated, then said, "It is not so simple as that, Marie Annette. Rippiers is a very old house. It dates back to the early part of the fifteenth century, when King Henry the Fourth bestowed privileges on certain persons for selling fish. They were called rippiers, and one of these prosperous fishermen built the house. But it did not come into my family's possession until my great-grandfather bought it after barely escaping with his life during the Revolution."

"There was revolution when my mother sent me to England."

"A small uprising. I speak of the Great Revolution, when almost all the aristocracy was wiped away. My great-grandmother lost her head, but Great-grandfather managed to save himself and his infant son, my grandfather."

"You speak of your grandfather and great-grandfather," Marie objected, "but they are also mine."

For a few minutes Alain seemed at a loss to know what to say. "Marie Annette—my dear little cousin—" He paused, then went on, "I call you cousin, but you are only my cousin by courtesy."

"What do you mean?"

"Why, that you were—How do you say it?—that you were born on the—on the wrong side of the blanket."

"Do you call me bastard?" Marie cried, angrily. "I have told you that my father married my mother, legally and honestly."

"What proof have you?"

"My mother's letter."

"Pooh!" He made a gesture of brushing it aside. "What proof is that? It is the defence of a poor servant girl against her shame."

"Somewhere the marriage must be recorded."

"Perhaps. But where? For fifty years and more France was unsettled. The spirit of revolution smouldered, like a fire that could at any moment flare up, and added to this there was the war with England. Documents were lost, or were burnt by those who changed their politics and wished to forget what they had been. How would you begin such a search? Where would you find the money to engage lawyers and advocates? Forget it, Marie Annette. Do not fight me."

She stared at him, astounded. "Fight you? Why should I fight you? I have no quarrel with you." She stopped, then added, timidly, "I thought you were my friend."

"So I am." He laid his hand over hers. "It is as a friend that I advise you to give up all thought of establishing your legitimacy."

Marie shivered, despite the warmth of the day, for it occurred to her that if she had no right to anything pertaining to the Vaudelets she was still a pauper, a penniless girl who might be forced to re-enact the course her mother had taken. She could well follow that same path, could be turned away from her family home, or tolerated there as a servant.

Rippiers sat snugly in a lush valley to the north-west of Rye. Between the trees of the park could be seen Rye on its rock, like a look-out on guard against any danger which might approach by sea.

The coachman would have driven straight into the town but Alain directed him to turn left into a narrow road, and, a mile or so further on, to enter a drive between a pair of open iron gates, one of which leaned crookedly from a broken hinge. Inside the gates was a small lodge, but, as far as Marie could judge, it was empty.

The drive was flanked by a twenty-foot high wall of shrubs which consisted of rhododendron, laurel and holly, all requiring cutting and pruning. It was a pity, she thought, that whoever had planted them had chosen such dark and sad-looking bushes and, moreover, that the shrubs had been allowed to encroach on the path so considerably that branchlets scraped the sides of the carriage.

"What a long distance the house is from the road."

"It is safer that way. My great-grandfather was pleased. Perhaps that is why he bought it."

"Was he fearful of robbers, then?"

"He thought he might be followed from the Continent, and himself and his son murdered. He had enemies. Well, a French aristocrat of an old titled family would be fortunate indeed if he did *not* have enemies."

"I'm glad I have no enemies."

He glanced at her. Was she indeed so naïve, or had she spoken mockingly? "Everyone has enemies."

His expression was sombre. He did not look like a man who was coming to the place which had been his family's home for sixty years or so.

As if his frame of mind had been contagious, Marie found herself becoming depressed, almost apprehensive. The park was unkempt, its grass coarse and rough, the dead branches of some of its trees projecting gracelessly from among the green leaves, while others had snapped and hung down, held only by the bark and swinging slightly in the wind.

The bordering shrubs ceased suddenly, and there was the house about a quarter of a mile away. It might have been an abbey church or a monastery, for it had tall Gothic windows, pillars which ran the length of the facade as straight and uncompromising as soldiers on parade, and from each corner of the roof spires pointed to the sky. No building could have presented a greater contrast to the Leather Bottle, yet for a moment Marie was aware of a longing for that miserable tavern in Wapping.

She stifled her feelings, and turned to Alain. "It is beautiful."

He shrugged his shoulders. "Not a bad little place, but you should have seen our chateau."

"Was it larger than this?"

"This? This could have been set down in the courtyard."

"How could you bear to leave it?"

"It was taken from us. Now, no doubt, it is the residence of some linen-draper or corn-dealer."

Marie was puzzled. "You could have returned sooner."

"My father and uncle did not care for England. They were

happy when the Reign of Terror was over and they could go back to France."

"But you came to school in England."

"That was my mother's wish. Now my parents are both dead and I can please myself."

They stopped, and Alain handed her from the carriage. This was to be her home, and she must grow to love it. Never mind its somewhat grim exterior. Inside would be light and luxury. She visualised it as the hotel in Brighton, that being the only handsome building she had ever entered.

Alain strode between two of the pillars to a massive oaken door and pulled the rusty handle of a bell. No sound resulted, but he found himself holding the handle, from which a length of broken wire twisted like a snake.

With an exclamation of disgust he strode to the cab, took out his silver-headed stick and hammered fiercely on the door.

The door opened a few inches and Alain pushed it, almost knocking over the person who stood behind it. There was the sound of voices. Marie waited. The coachman was standing stolidly at the horses' heads. It seemed a long time before Alain came out.

"You can take the horses round to the stables," he said, to the coachman. "I'll send a man to show you where everything is. Come, Marie Annette, you must be tired." He spoke so kindly that she was reassured. Of course the broken bell had made him angry. He had wanted everything to be perfect. But it was a trifling matter, one which could easily be put right.

He motioned to her to enter, and she moved forward through the door and into the hall. The light was dim, for though an enormous window reached almost from floor to ceiling, it was of stained glass, its colours so deep that red and blue patches checkered the furnishings and the wall and those who were present.

Besides Alain and herself, Marie saw only two people, whom Alain introduced as "Mr and Mrs Mumby".

She smiled and murmured a greeting, trying not to stare too closely, too rudely. The man and the woman before her did not move or speak. They might have been wax figures, and they were old, as old as anyone Marie had ever known. Not even in Wapping, not even begging in the shadows, not even waiting outside the workhouse had she seen two more decrepit and wretched creatures.

TWO

Alain was angry. He threw out his arm towards the old couple and said to Marie, "You see? Mumby by name and mum by nature." He strode up and down as he talked, stopping each time he reached the man and woman, and raising his stick as if he were in half a mind to thump their heads with the silver knob. "I arrive here and what do I find? I am not expected. Scarcely can I gain entrance through my own door. Have you provided food for us? Are the rooms prepared? Come, speak! Are you dumb?"

The old man began to shake. His head nodded, and as he raised his hands in what looked like an appeal, they fluttered as leaves in a wind. "Well?" Alain shouted, and the servant cleared his throat with a rasping sound. "We did not know, master."

"What did you not know?"

"That you were coming."

"I sent word to you. I wrote a letter. Where is it?"

"There was no letter, master. I never seen one."

As though this were a cue, the old woman lifted her skirt, disclosing a red flannel petticoat, and plunged her hand into the folds, from which she drew an envelope and waved it triumphantly.

Alain snatched it from her. "Parbleu! Not even opened. What is the use of an unopened letter?"

"It wouldn't be no use if it was opened," the old man explained, apologetically. "She can't read."

"Can you read?"

"Yes, master, I can read print. I'm not so good to

understand pen-work, with the loops and the curls and so on."

"Why didn't your wife give you the letter?"

"She's afeared of letters, and she don't much hold with them, believing as they mostly bring bad news."

Alain snorted. "There will be bad news for you unless you stir yourselves. Mrs Mumby, you had better take yourself off to the kitchen and prepare some food, if there is any fit for eating."

They went about their business, moving with what was for them some haste, though that was little more than a snail's pace. The old man stopped and turned before he had crossed the hall. "We thought you was all dead," he quavered.

"My mother and father are dead and so is my uncle," Alain told him, "but you will find that I am very much alive, and," he added, grimly, "exceedingly hungry."

The old man shuffled off, shaking his head, and Marie said, "They are afraid of you."

"And so they should be. They are a useless pair, not fit to be caretakers of a dog-kennel."

He looked extremely handsome, Marie thought, as he stood with legs apart, tapping his stick against his boots, his face slightly flushed with anger. She should, she supposed, take exception to Alain's overbearing manner, but she could not seriously do so. He was a gentleman, and gentlemen were born to rule.

"Have they been here long?" she asked. Alain glanced at her inquiringly, and she added, "The Mumbys."

"Oh! For ever. Or practically for ever. My grandfather left them here when we returned to France. He made arrangements for an English lawyer to pay them their regular wages and keep. That was twenty years ago. They must have been less stupid at that time."

He looked round the hall, which was bare and chilly. The walls showed patches where once pictures had hung. There were no pieces of furniture, no rugs upon the floor. "What a barn this is! Let us see how the rest of the house fares."

He walked to the end of the hall and threw open a pair of massive doors. "If I remember rightly, this was the drawing-room."

Marie followed him. The room was almost as bleak as the hall. A long refectory table was the memorial to past banquets but no chairs remained for the seating of guests. A large wrought-iron chandelier hung crookedly from the ceiling. The only object of beauty was an ornate mantelpiece in coloured marbles, over which hung a coat-of-arms, its gilt tarnished, its paint peeling.

Impatiently Alain turned and went out, crossing the hall to the staircase, and Marie followed him.

Upstairs was the great drawing-room. This was furnished, but everything was shrouded in dust-sheets. Ivy had crept across the long windows, obscuring much of the daylight.

Alain lifted the covering from a sofa. The satin upholstery was in rags, and among the stuffing were the remains of a mouse's nest. "Faugh!" he exclaimed. "It would cost a fortune to restore this place."

"But you will do it?" She spoke anxiously, and then wondered why it should matter so much to her.

"I shall do a great deal," he answered, briskly. "I have many plans. But now let us find a room which is sufficiently tolerable to be your sleeping-chamber."

She thought she might be given a choice of quarters, but Alain made the decision, and she could find no cause for complaint. Almost anything would have been comfortable after her room in Wapping, and this was luxury, albeit shabby luxury. The bed, so large that Marie felt she might lose herself in it, was of brass, dulled by damp and neglect; the hangings and coverlets were of crimson silk, faded in places to old rose, and the long curtains at the windows matched the bed-furnishings. There was a linen-press in mahogany, an oak armoire carved with shields and fleurs-de-lis, two chairs, and a table on which stood a swinging mirror. The walls showed signs of damp, and the ceiling, which had once been painted, was rough and flaking.

"A fire shall be lighted," Alain said, abruptly, and turned and left without another word.

It took Marie but a few minutes to unfasten her small bundle and lay away her few possessions, and then she wondered what next to do.

She was about to go in search of Alain when Mr Mumby arrived with the equipment for making the fire. She offered to help him, but he appeared to be so distressed at the idea that she desisted.

The fire gave life and cheerfulness to the room. Marie sat beside it, gazing at the flames, her restlessness soothed. The journey had tired her and she was dropping into a light doze when the door opened and Mr Mumby announced, "There's food served. 'Tis in the next room."

Gladly she jumped to her feet and followed him, realising she was indeed hungry.

Alain was already seated at a table, and as soon as he spoke she knew with relief that he was in a better mood. "Come, Marie, let us feast, though heaven knows feast is a word far from appropriate for describing it. This roasted creature is a hare, Mrs Mumby tells me, trapped on the estate."

"It smells good," Marie said.

"The bread is fit only for peasants, so dark is it, and I suspect the cheese to be made from goat's milk. Well, Marie, are you prepared to eat it?"

"Oh, yes, please!"

"Then I also will take the risk. The wine I can with safety recommend. My grandfather left it when we returned to France."

Whatever Alain might think of the food, Marie found it delicious, and when she had eaten she felt refreshed, and the house no longer seemed cold and frightening and hostile.

"I like this room."

He smiled in agreement. "I suspect the Mumbys used it and kept it aired and dry. It shall be both our sitting-room and dining-room until I have had time to put the rest of the place in order."

"There are books. May I read them?"

"Of course! But these are few. Wait until you have seen the library, though I warrant most of the books will be rotted and worm-eaten. Now, Marie, we will retire early. Tomorrow I go to Rye to make arrangements with the tradesmen to supply us with food and other necessities, and from there I continue to London."

She stared at him, surprised and alarmed. "You are going away?"

"Yes, I have matters to which I must attend. My father died so recently that I do not know the state of his affairs in England. I shall consult with the lawyers, and when I have received their report I will engage builders to come down and commence the renovations necessary for Rippiers."

"Take me with you!" Marie cried, impulsively.

He laughed. "Why, you foolish girl, I have just brought you from London, have I not? You have escaped. Does the prisoner crave to return to her prison?"

She shivered. "Of course not! I never wish to see Wapping again. But I could go with you, be with you, and I should be safe."

"No, no! It is impossible. It would not be fitting to take a young girl on such business as I have to transact. Besides, it would be dull for you."

"I am sure it would not." She clasped her hands. "Please, Alain, do not leave me."

"Marie, there is nothing here to harm you. I cannot understand why suddenly you have become so timid. You were brave enough when that dreadful woman confined you to that miserable cell."

"It was different. That was my bedroom. I was accustomed to it."

"As you will grow accustomed to Rippiers. Now be a good girl, and let me hear no more complaints."

She knew she could not move him. "How long will you be gone?" she asked, faintly.

He shrugged his shoulders. "How can I tell? Perhaps two weeks. Perhaps three or four."

She was dismayed. "So long?"

"It will seem like no time at all. The days will fly past."

"Here there are no people."

"When you become used to the country you will wonder how you ever endured London, the fog lying low in the damp weather and the dust and chaff and straw blowing in the dry weather. You are a fortunate young lady, Marie. Now go to bed and have sweet dreams."

But for several hours she had no dreams. She lay awake wondering what she should do. Could she present Alain with an ultimatum, threaten to run away if he did not allow her to accompany him? But would he care if she did run away? Why had he brought her here, anyway? Had he rescued her from sheer charity, sheer humanity, or had he some use for her? But what use could she be to him?

She did not know what time it was when she awoke, but she sprang straight from bed and dressed hastily and went into the study and found it empty, with no sign that breakfast had been taken. Perhaps it was earlier than she thought.

Downstairs she went, to the hall, which was almost as much in twilight this summer's morning as it had been on the previous day. Where the kitchen was she did not know, and the first two passages she followed led only to empty rooms or to doors leading outside. Persevering, however, she came at last to the kitchen, where by a large range in which was a blazing fire sat Mrs Mumby sipping something from a cup.

Marie greeted her brightly. "Good morning! I am looking for Monsieur Vaudelet."

The old woman did not reply. Perhaps she did not think an answer was required to something which after all was not a question.

Marie tried again. "Where is Monsieur Vaudelet?"

Mrs Mumby stared at her, and Marie began to wonder

whether in truth the old woman was dumb. So far she had not spoken a word.

But Mrs Mumby dispelled the doubt. She took the cup from her mouth, and smacked her lips, and said, "He's gone."

THREE

Marie's first sensation was one of sheer panic, of being trapped. Not since she had been locked in the cellar of the Leather Bottle had she been stricken with such a sense of horror and dread. She told herself that she was free to come and go as she wished, that the whole world was there, outside. Should she desire to leave, no locked doors would confront her. There was no-one to force her to do anything against her will.

In vain she argued with herself. Her assurances made no headway against her fear. One morning when Alain had been away for four days she stood at the window of the study. The sun was already high in a sky of tranquil blue. She should have been looking out on a morning of summer pleasure. What she saw was a small pond set in a grassy clearing surrounded by trees. At the edge of it was a stone statue of a naked boy. In his right hand, away from his mouth, he held panpipes. His left forearm was missing and his nose was chipped. The pond was covered with thick scum, and on the boy's body were patches of green moss and brownish lichen.

She moved away in impatience. The simple facts were that Alain had left her alone in a dilapidated house with a pair of old people out of whom she would be lucky to extract one word of conversation.

Viewed in this light, her fear was irrational. There was really a great deal to do. Alain had not forbidden her anything. She could explore the house and the grounds and the surrounding countryside, could even walk into Rye if she wished.

Strengthened, by these sensible thoughts, she decided to go for a walk, so she went to her room and put on her bonnet. There was no need for her paletot on such a warm morning. In fact, her alpaca dress was too heavy for the time of the year, and she found herself wishing she had a muslin gown.

She went to find the Mumbys, to tell them she was going out, but they were nowhere to be seen, so she abandoned the idea.

The sun was not too hot, for there was a slight refreshing breeze, and she felt her spirits rising. Through the grass she ran until she was out of breath, then threw herself down and lay back and looked up at the sky and sang a song.

When she had rested, she sat up. Distance diminished the house. From here it looked far less overpowering. What was it after all, but a heap of stone piled up in the middle of a park?

She jumped up and peered around for some flowers to put in her bonnet, but there were none. Everything was green except the trunks of the trees, and they were a dreary brown. Had no one ever cared to grow flowers? Even in Wapping there were flowers, on the stalls and in the market.

She took off her bonnet and unpinned her hair. Now she was like a child again, plain and undignified, but what did it matter, when there was no one to see? The wind stirred her hair deliciously, and she continued on her way, swinging her bonnet.

Presently the tall oaks and chestnuts gave place to holly and hawthorn which closed in, forming a coppice, and there was an undergrowth of low shrubs and of brambles which caught at her skirt. Here it was not so pleasant to walk, and she was half inclined to turn back, but a kind of curiosity led her to wish to discover what lay beyond. She followed a path, but then it narrowed and finally disappeared, and she stopped, dismayed. Which way now? Better to retrace her steps, but when she looked behind her she was not sure from which direction she had come.

The wise course seemed to be to go forward, and when the

wood ended she would be able to get her bearings. Doggedly
she kept on, nettles waist high, brambles whipping about her
ankles to trip her, until it seemed that this wilderness was
unending, and she became really frightened. Yet to go back
now seemed as difficult as to continue.

She was becoming desperate when suddenly the ground
ahead was free of obstacles and she was in a clearing. The
trees made a circle round it, so that the sun scarcely touched
it, and in the centre of it was a hut, a hovel of a building not
worthy of the name of cottage, yet obviously a dwelling-place.
Drunkenly it leaned on its rotting timbers, and its thatch was
so green and overgrown that it resembled a tree rather than a
house.

But it was not this hut which first caught Marie's eye. Her
attention was attracted by a line which stretched from side to
side of the clearing, upheld by several poles. At first Marie
took this to be a clothes-line furnished with washing, until
she saw with what grisly objects it was decked. Here were the
skins and corpses of creatures of the wild, a fox-pelt complete
with fine brush, a badger skin, tiny mole-skins, all fastened to
the line, and hanging from strings were the bodies of weasel
and crow, magpie and kite and pigeon in various stages of
decomposition, down to the very skeleton.

Marie turned away, feeling sick, unable to face this
horrible sight. Yet face it she must, if she intended to seek
someone to show her the way out of this baffling maze.

Gathering courage from her necessity she began to cross
the clearing, keeping her eyes from the gruesome row of
relics.

She knocked on the door of the hut, and even the gentle tap
of her knuckles sounded loud in the hush of the clearing. It
occurred to her, with some surprise, that it was strange no
birds should be singing. Could it be that the wholesale
murder of their kind was apparent to them, so that they
shunned the gallows and its surroundings?

The door remained closed and there was no sound of
anyone stirring within. She knocked again, but without hope,

for in so small a place her first summons would surely have been heard. Suddenly the silence seemed more oppressive, the emptiness more universal.

Driven by curiosity, she could not resist peeping through the window. The room would have been too dark to show any detail had there not been a hole in the roof which let in a shaft of light. This light fell full on a table and chair. The table was laid for a rough meal. There was a loaf of bread, and on a plate were lumps of some kind of meat. The chair was occupied by a man who was eating, and as Marie gazed in astonishment the man raised his head, and it was no man. It was Peter!

Peter looked her full in the face, and an icy chill froze Marie's body. She could not move. She felt she would never move again.

Peter sprang to her feet, knocking over the chair, and Marie found that she was running, running towards the trees, which no longer were obstacles but a sanctuary.

She could hear Peter's feet thudding behind her, and she knew that somehow she must outpace her pursuer, though how she could expect to do so was beyond her imagination. Peter was strong, would have the protection of trousers and heavy boots. Marie had the inconvenience of a long, full skirt which the brambles caught and held, slowing her down. What Peter would do to her she had no idea, she only knew she must run, in a blind instinct to preserve her life.

Her lungs felt as though they would burst, her hair dragged across her eyes so that she could not see the twigs which whipped back, stinging her face. She became aware of the futility of her wild flight. Soon, very soon now, she would fall exhausted to the ground, and then it would be over.

The trees and bushes showed no sign of thinning. It was, indeed, becoming more difficult to force her way between them. Peter was drawing closer. Marie could hear loud breathing, and it was only the thickness of the woodland growth which prevented them from being visible to each other.

She was at the end of her strength. Her legs would no longer obey her, and so painful was it to breathe that the prospect of ceasing to move was as sweet as heaven, and her fear of Peter seemed of little importance.

On her left was a thick clump of rhododendron. She sensed rather than saw it, and stopped abruptly, flinging herself towards it, tripping and falling into that green wall. She pressed her face to the ground, that her gasps might not be heard, and the sound of Peter's feet went past her and faded into the distance.

When she could move, which was not for some time, she crawled more deeply into the darkness of her shelter. The rhododendrons were old and untended, and after the manner of their species they sent out long branches towards the light, creating a thick, leafless tangle of twisted wood. Marie crept toward the root of that particular bush which had formed a slight hollow spongy with fallen leaves. Into this she burrowed, as a sick animal might have done, and lay motionless.

After a time Peter returned. She had evidently come to the conclusion that Marie had eluded her, for she moved slowly, searching the sides of the path they had made.

When she reached the rhododendrons she lifted the lower branches and peered beneath them. Had Marie remained in her first hiding-place she would inevitably have been caught, but the hollow was some fifteen feet away, and she was half buried by the leaves, half hidden by the gnarled roots, so that in the dimness she was invisible.

Peter gave up at last, and went away, but it was another hour or two before Marie dared or cared to move. She was stiff and exhausted, and could only stumble slowly along. How to get out of the wood she did not know, but somehow this did not seem to matter any more. Her only desire was to escape from Peter, to go in a direction which would not lead her again to the clearing.

From time to time she stopped, partly to rest, and partly to listen, tense and terrified, for those footsteps. There was no

sound of them, and in this part of the wood the birds were
singing, and suddenly a shaft of sunlight struck through the
trees, and there was the earth and the sky, open and inviting.

She ran the last few steps, and then sank down sobbing
with exhaustion and relief. She had come out further down
the valley. Rippiers peeped through its trees, about a mile
away.

That was the longest mile Marie had ever walked. Her
legs ached and her feet were blistered. What she would wear
she did not know, for this, her only dress, was torn in a dozen
places. Her bonnet she had dropped somewhere on her flight.

Though the sunshine and the open landscape gave an
illusion of safety, she kept glancing at the woods on her left.
If Peter emerged from them what would prevent her from
making an attack here, where there was no one to help?

But Peter did not appear, and Marie began to move more
quickly as she drew nearer to the house. At that moment
Rippiers appeared beautiful, not shabby, not sinister. It was
a refuge from danger. She believed it to be a refuge from
death.

In the drive outside the great doors stood a carriage. Marie
started to run. It must be Alain had returned. It must be that
he had changed his mind and decided after all to take her
with him.

She burst into the hall, excited and expectant. But it was
not Alain who waited there. It was a little lady, and at her
feet was a pile of boxes.

FOUR

"Oh!" It was all Marie could find to say, just "Oh!" It expressed her complete astonishment, which made her oblivious to her wildly dishevelled appearance, the torn hem of her dress trailing, the bodice ripped and snagged, her tangled hair threaded with twigs and leaves, her face smudged with moss and soil. A third time she said, "Oh!" because it was difficult to believe in Peter and the hut and the chase. How could fear and danger exist in the same world as this small lady, dressed with the most impeccable neatness and taste, who stood calmly in the middle of the bare hall, surrounded by baskets and bandboxes?

Even when she gazed at Marie, the visitor's composure remained unbroken. "I can see you have been for a long country walk," she observed.

Marie clutched at a strip of bodice which was revealing her camisole. "Yes, I—yes, the brambles are thorny."

"Brambles usually are. It is wise that you wore old clothes for your expedition."

Marie looked down at the ruin of her dress, her only dress. What should she do? What in heaven's name could she do? First, however, since she was in Alain's absence the hostess, she must establish the identity of this person.

"Are you a friend of Monsieur Vaudelet?"

"I would not presume to call the Marquis a friend," the lady said, severely. "I am here to serve him. Allow me to introduce myself. Miss Mary Grey, court dressmaker."

"I'm Marie." At the Leather Bottle that would have been sufficient, but here—"Marie Annette Madeleine Veronique

Vaudelet." She drew herself up as she spoke, and the tattered dress did not seem so important.

"Ah, then you are the young lady. The Marquis called a few days ago and asked me to wait upon you."

"From Rye?"

"That is where my business is situated."

"Have you come to stay?"

Miss Grey permitted herself a smile. "My business would scarcely prosper were I to desert it. No, today we merely have to choose styles and materials, and I will take your measurements."

Marie's mouth opened and remained open. She could think of nothing to say, and Miss Grey, seeing her difficulty, continued kindly, "I will do my best to oblige you. The Marquis instructed me to provide you with a complete wardrobe."

Coming on top of her recent fearful experience, it was too much to assimilate at once. She could only point out, artlessly, "He isn't really a marquis now, you know."

Miss Grey was shocked, and showed it. "In England, I am glad to say, we still have respect for the Almighty and the nobility. Will you ring for a servant to carry the boxes to your room?"

Vaguely Marie looked round. "I am not sure—I think the bell-pulls have been removed. Shall I—" She went towards the boxes.

"Certainly not!" Miss Grey exclaimed.

"Then I will try to find Mr Mumby."

She hurried away and managed to run him to ground, but there was so much baggage that she surreptitiously loaded herself with four hat-boxes as she brought up the rear, and Miss Grey, ascending the staircase majestically in front, either did not notice or else made no comment.

Once in Marie's room, the dressmaker wasted no time. Ribbons and straps were unfastened, lids removed, and fabrics foamed into the room like an incoming tide. There was satin and velvet and gauze and brocaded silk. There were trimmings of lace and jet and mother-of-pearl and embroidered braid inset with feathers of humming-birds. Marie was overawed, but Miss Grey treated them with a casualness almost amounting to contempt, snatching up a length of silk tarlatane woven with strips of glittering gold, and flinging it over Marie's shoulder to see whether the colour became her.

"You are fortunate to be young. For the young there is nothing more charming than the new satin-striped poplin petticoats, with the dress looped up at the sides to show the petticoat."

Marie picked up some filmy muslin, pink as a sunset cloud. "This is pretty."

"Not with your hair," Miss Grey said, decisively. "Leave that for the yellow-haired, blue-eyed misses. Now here is something I will create for you. Black velvet over a petticoat of black and orange bordered with a deep jet trimming. The sleeves shall be lined with orange and the bodice fastened with large gold buttons." She glanced up sternly at Marie. "I shall not pander to the low-cut French fashions. Monsieur Talleyrand remarked of a dress that it began too late and ended too soon. But no doubt you have heard that."

"No, I haven't," Marie confessed, and reflected that she seemed to have heard very little about anything.

"You need a hairdresser," Miss Grey observed. "Unless you wear a chignon you cannot be à la mode. Fortunately your hair is thick. You will not need to load your head with the weight of a pound or two of dyed sheep's wool."

For hours the conference continued, until Marie begged leave to go and instruct Mrs Mumby to prepare a meal.

"Well," Miss Grey conceded, "I could take a little something before returning to Rye. Of course this is only a preliminary visit. There will need to be several fittings." She paused, and added, "I hope you have no objection."

"Oh, no! No, I shall be pleased to see you." She spoke with sincere feeling, for Miss Grey was a symbol of safety, a link with the ordinary outside world. She was reluctant to let the little lady go, and would have begged her to remain for the night had she not known it would be useless to do so.

She stood in the drive as the boxes were piled on to the carriage and Miss Grey climbed in and waved and the coachman started off. The place was suddenly very empty, very lonely. She looked up at the line of trees where the wood edged the valley. There was no knowing who might be watching from that green fortress. She shivered, and went into the house and locked and bolted the heavy doors, wondering whether what she did was any protection.

She felt a pressing need to talk to someone, and obviously there was no one except the Mumbys. With Mrs Mumby it had so far been impossible to communicate in words of more than one syllable, but the old man was slightly more sociable, if such a term could be used with regard to either of the couple.

The opportunity came when she found him opening the main doors on the following morning. "You're not going to leave the doors open, are you, Mr Mumby?"

He nodded abruptly, and replied, "I am."

"Don't you think you should keep them locked?"

He clasped his hands and looked at her from under his furry white eyebrows. "After the place is aired. Must be aired every morning."

"I see." She was so relieved that she felt friendliness towards him. "I am glad you lock the doors. I think you should push the bolts as well."

"No, no!" He seemed irritated by her ignorance. "Bolts is for night."

He turned to go, and she followed him. "Mr Mumby-"

Reluctantly he stopped.

"Mr Mumby, I want to ask you something. Is there anyone else here? I mean, anyone besides you and Mrs Mumby."

His hands began to shake, which Marie judged to be a sign that he was nervous and distressed. "Nobody. Nobody at all. Just the two."

"You'll be glad when Monsieur Vaudelet engages a proper staff."

He spun round to face her, and it was as if a wax figure had suddenly come to life. "No, no! He mustn't!"

"But you need help. There's too much work for you, at your age."

He trembled so violently that Marie expected to hear his teeth chattering. "Never the workhouse!"

"Who mentioned the workhouse?"

"It would kill Mrs Mumby. We've nowhere else to go."

"Monsieur Vaudelet would not turn you out."

"They always do. They send you away. There's no place for the old."

"I wouldn't let them do it. I promise you."

"You?"

Like inspiration a thought occurred to her. "Mr Mumby, you have been here a long time. Do you remember a girl, she was a servant, a girl called Jane?"

"Ah! Went to France with them she did."

"Well, I am her daughter."

If she expected any expression of surprise or pleasure she was to be disappointed. Mr Mumby wished to get away. The conversation had agitated him, put him in a fluster, and this he did not like.

"Tell me about her!" Marie insisted.

"Who?"

"My mother."

Mr Mumby was silent, seeming to be meditating, and at last he said, "She was a good girl."

"Is that all?. He did not reply, but turned to go, and Marie quickly asked the question which concerned her particularly at the moment. "Who lives in the hut?"

"Hut?"

"Yes. The one in the middle of the wood."

He scratched his head. "Hm! Ah! Hut. That'll be the gamekeeper's house."

"A poor sort of house."

"And a poor sort of man."

"But he protects the estate." Marie was suddenly cheerful, as if she felt herself to be protected. "If he found a stranger in his hut, or in the woods, he'd turn that person out, wouldn't he? He'd never allow trespassers."

"Nay, nay! He'll not allow nor forbid any more. He's dead. Caught in one of his own traps he was, and a good riddance!"

Marie's heart sank. The sense of protection evaporated all too quickly. Once again the woods were foreign territory, bristling with danger.

The summer days were long and warm and sunny, but Marie did not dare to venture more than twenty or thirty yards from the house. In vain she reasoned with herself, reminding herself that Peter had willingly let her go with Alain, had been well paid to do so. No, something had happened to cause her to desire to secure her captive once more, and Marie was certain Peter would stick at nothing in order to do so.

So Marie strolled in the sun, solitary and watchful. It was not an enlivening way to take the air, and the hours passed slowly. Not for many days could she expect Alain's return. It was only Miss Grey on whom she could depend to relieve the monotony, and as she paced the drive and the neglected lawns her eyes and ears were strained to see and hear a carriage approaching.

FIVE

Miss Grey set her seamstresses to work, and engaged extra hands, and had the garments ready for the first fitting in a few days.

It was sooner than Marie had dared hope, and she greeted Miss Grey with a welcome beyond that usually extended by a lady to her dressmaker.

The visits, therefore, were a pleasure to both of them, and Marie found her fears becoming less acute. It was foolish, she decided, to suppose that Peter would show herself in the open, would come right down to the house. Peter would not know how many servants there were, would not expect such a residence to be left in the care of two old helpless people like the Mumbys.

How easy it was, Marie thought, to see things in a practical, sensible light when she was chatting with the dressmaker. Not so easy, though, was it to be brave when the dressmaker paid her last visit.

"Are you sure everything is finished?" she asked.

Miss Grey laughed. She could not believe Marie was serious. Had she not brought the hairdresser with her on one of the trips, the milliner on another, the shoemaker on a third? Did not the well-stocked cupboards bear witness to the magnitude of her task? Would not the bill, when she presented it to the Marquis, be an even more potent witness?

"I shall miss you," Marie said, miserably.

Miss Grey was not sentimental. She spoke briskly. "We have been acquainted for less than four weeks. I am sure you will not suffer any heartache at my absence. I feel I have supplied you with everything for every occasion."

"Oh, yes, indeed! I am most grateful."

This, Miss Grey felt, was putting gratitude in the wrong place. She was the one who should be grateful.

"So we must say goodbye," she told Marie, lightly.

In desperation Marie tried another ploy. "If there should be anything requiring alteration—"

"I don't believe there will be,but if there should, then you can send a message to me."

"How? I'm sure the Mumbys could never walk as far as town."

"Then perhaps you could yourself ride over."

"The stables are empty, and anyway I have not learned to ride on horseback."

"Well—" Miss Grey found herself in something of a quandary. She was a busy woman and could not be expected to be responsible for a grown-up young lady. All the same she could not help feeling sorry for the lonely little creature.

"Look," she said, "the Marquis is certain to come home within the next few days. If, in the meantime, any emergency should arise, you can come to me. The walk to Rye would present no obstacle to you. But I am certain there will be no necessity to resort to such an expedient."

With this Marie had to be satisfied, though she was far from happy at the prospect of the lonely days ahead, and the uncertainty of the time of Alain's return.

To pass the time indoors she read many books, both those in the study, and a few from the library, though these too often were crumbling or unpleasantly stained with damp.

But when she lifted her head from her reading she would see the sunshine striking through the dusty windows and would decide it was not bookish weather, and then she would go out, stifling the fear which still beset her.

The stables were at the back of the house, and since mentioning them to Miss Grey it had struck her that to explore them would offer some variety in the short distance she allowed herself to venture out. In order to reach them she passed through a narrow belt of trees which went down to a small stream and then rose on the far side. It was the first time she had moved out of sight of the windows and doors of the house since her dreadful experience in the woods, but once she had ventured she lost her nervousness. There was another way to the stables, which horses and carriages used, but that was by the drive, and was much further, and who would take the trouble, she thought, almost defiantly. The stables, though empty and swept clean, were reassuring in their atmosphere of familiar things and their warm, lingering smell of horses.

It became her habit to spend an hour or so each day in this part of Rippiers, going in and out by one of the kitchen doors, and as she paced the flagged courtyard in front of the stables she would make plans for the future, such as asking Alain to buy her a horse and teaching her to ride.

One morning as she strolled through the stables she amused herself by choosing where her mount should be housed, and deciding on a name for him.

She was so deep in thought that when she heard a sound she did not for a moment connect it with anything around her, but vaguely ascribed it to the wind.

It came again, and would have meant nothing had the stables been in use, for it was the kind of sound which might come from a horse's bridle as it shook its head.

Marie stayed motionless. It was the wind. It must be. But there was no wind. The day was too still for the fluttering of the smallest leaf.

A little further along was the harness room, where some of the old leathers and girths still hung. The noise had seemed to come from there. It would be a mouse or a rat, Marie told herself. She was not afraid of such vermin. Rats there had been in plenty in Wapping, down by the river.

With thumping heart she moved towards the harness-room. She did not expect to find anything, she assured herself, but she had to know that the room was empty save for the animals who had taken it for their habitation.

At the side of the door was a small window, spattered with

dried rain-drops on the outside, criss-crossed with spiders' webs on the inside. As she drew level with it she turned her head and looked in, almost involuntarily. There was a face, a face peering out, pressed so closely to the pane that it was flattened and distorted.

Marie gave a cry, and found she was running with scarcely an awareness of the motion. It was almost as if she flew through the air. "Peter!" The name thudded through her mind and from her very heart. She had not seen the face properly, had given it no more than the briefest of glances, could not with any certainty have recognised it through that begrimed window. Yet she had no doubt at all, would have sworn upon her very life that it was Peter who had descended upon Rippiers, was besieging the fortress itself.

She did not know whether Peter was following her, did not pause for an instant to look over her shoulder, but plunged through the trees, half sliding down the grassy slope, intent only upon reaching the house.

With one stride she was across the short plank bridging the stream, and was climbing the slope on the other side. Here the moisture fed the grass, keeping it long and lush, so that it lay across the path, almost obliterating it, but by now Marie knew every step of the way and was surprised when she stumbled over some obstacle where no obstacle should be. It was a stone, she supposed, and she would not have checked her headlong flight if the obstacle had not, at that moment, groaned.

She looked down. A man was lying across the path. He was unconscious, or nearly so, and the grass around him was seeped in blood. The shock of the sight stopped her, even while her instinct to reach safety urged her forward. She alone could do nothing for this man, would not have the strength to move him.

She ran on and burst into the kitchen, where fortunately were both Mumbys, and attempted to make them understand what had happened. It was not easy, for she was out of breath, and it was an effort for them to digest such an extraordinary piece of news. They must bring the man to the house, she insisted, must carry him on some kind of stretcher, perhaps a rug on a hurdle would answer the purpose.

It took all her courage to go out there, to resist an impulse to hang back behind the Mumbys. So quiet was it under the trees that she suspected an ambush, and she stiffened, ears strained to catch the slightest sound.

There was no sign of Peter, and the man lay there, this time without moving or uttering the faintest moan. Shakily Mr Mumby knelt down and laid his ear against the man's chest. "He's alive, just, but he's lost a lot of blood."

Now Marie was all haste. So far they had been fortunate, but there was no guarantee that they were safe. They must hurry, return to shelter without delay.

She said it aloud. "We must hurry."

It was as if the Mumbys did not understand the word. With the deliberation of a pair of tortoises they set about laying down the hurdle, and then they surveyed the man as though they were calculating how they might move a mountain.

"Oh, be quick! Be quick!" Marie cried. Her youth gave her strength equal to both of theirs, and she helped lift him on to the hurdle and cover him with the rug.

"He's been shot," Mr Mumby said.

"Who would do such a thing?" Marie spoke automatically, it being what she might be expected to ask, but in truth she believed only one person could be responsible.

The Mumbys made no attempt to answer the question, and slowly, stumblingly, they made their way back to the house. So great was Marie's relief when the door closed behind them and she had, unseen by the Mumbys, locked and bolted it, that she felt ready to face anything which might happen.

"We must remove his clothing, put him to bed, bathe his wound."

"Not you." It was Mrs Mumby, the silent one, who spoke.

Marie frowned, perplexed. "But I must help. You cannot manage alone."

"Not you," Mrs Mumby repeated. She stood beside the hurdle in an aggressive attitude, as though prepared to defend it with her life.

"Why not? If we don't do something soon, the man will die."

" 'Tain't fitting. A young girl."

Marie turned to Mr Mumby in exasperation. "What is she talking about?"

"She don't think it fitting that a young girl, specially a young lady, should undress a man. You go away and leave it to us, miss. We can do it. He's one of our kind."

"What makes you say that? Do you know him?"

"Ay. He be gamekeeper's son."

"The gamekeeper who was killed?"

"That's the one."

"Then he must live in the hut. He must know—"

It was no time to speculate on the significance of this piece of information. She said, sharply, "If you are going to attend to him you had better do so before it is too late."

She left the room, angry without quite knowing why. She supposed it was because she objected to being treated like a child or a delicate demoiselle liable to swoon at the sight of blood. Yet she was aware that her feeling ran deeper than this, for she had the impression that the Mumbys were keeping something from her. Was it possible that they were in some way involved with Peter? Was there no-one she could trust?

Restless and frightened she paced the hall, and it seemed ages before Mr Mumby emerged through the door from the domestic quarters. His face was as expressionless as usual, his movements as sluggish, but she sensed that he did not bring good news, and at the same time she asked herself, defiantly, what did it matter? What was it to her whether the man lived or died? Without him there might be one hazard the less to herself.

Mr Mumby stopped in front on her. "You'll have to fetch the doctor," he said. "He's in a bad way."

SIX

Marie stared at the old man. "Where is the nearest doctor?"

"In town."

"Then it's useless." The need to deny the feasibility of fetching a doctor was strong in her. "If the man is so badly wounded—"

"There's a bullet in him."

"—he'll be dead before the doctor can reach him. I don't think there is anything we can do." The words sounded callous, even in her own ears.

Mr Mumby had the pale, red-rimmed eyes of age. He blinked as he faced Marie, but he was not trembling now. He stood there firmly, obstinately, refusing to be denied. "We got to try to save him."

"We've done our best. We brought him into the house, and Mrs Mumby is tending him. There's no reason—"

"There's reason." Mr Mumby attempted to shout at her, but his voice merely rose to a squeak.

"What reason?"

The old man appeared to give up. His palsy took hold of him again, and he shook uncontrollably, muttering, "The doctor. The doctor."

Marie felt it should not be necessary to justify herself, but she could not resist it. "Don't you see? Someone out there shot him. Someone has a gun and would probably shoot us if we set foot outside. We must stay in the house, keep the doors locked."

"The doctor," Mr Mumby repeated.

Marie lost her temper. "Well, if you feel like that, why don't you go?"

He did not attempt to answer, just looked at her, and she was ashamed. Of course it was impossible for the old man to go. Even if he were capable of walking that distance without collapsing, he would take so long that the wounded man would certainly die before help arrived.

She drew a deep breath. "Very well. I will fetch the doctor." As she heard herself saying this, she was appalled. She must be mad. Peter was waiting for her. By what miracle could she expect to reach Rye? But now she was committed, and must scrape together such shreds of courage as remained to her.

The main drive led through the park to the highroad, which would be fairly well frequented and thus safer, but it was a mile or two longer than the direct way through the valley. For the sake of the injured man there was no choice but the short cut.

She walked as fast as she could, refusing to allow herself to break into a run, for if she did she would be exhausted before she reached the town, and unable to escape any threat which appeared later. She kept looking sideways at the dark line of the wood on the hill, and yet it was reasonable to suppose that Peter was still in the vicinity of the stables, where Marie had last seen her. As she went she found herself wondering when the man had been shot. It must have happened after she went to the stable yard, otherwise she would have seen him as she passed through the trees. But Peter was in the harness room. How long had she been there?

As she reflected on these problems, some of Marie's fear left her. The hill on which stood the town of Rye was drawing comfortingly closer. Soon she would be among people, and at that moment she wished she might never return to Rippiers.

She looked over her shoulder, and there behind her was Peter, striding along with the gait which so much more resembled that of a man than a woman. Marie increased her speed, and hoped she would not have to run, for then Peter would assuredly catch her, being stronger and more powerful.

When next she looked behind, Peter was gaining on her. Marie broke into a run. She was now very close to the outskirts of Rye. She could see the road in the distance, and desperation lent her the speed to reach it. Peter was drawing so near that Marie could hear her breathing. Another few yards and there would come a hand to clutch her and hold her in a grasp from which she would not be able to break free.

The road was just beyond the fence ahead, and she made one final intense effort. Peter must have stumbled on a tussock of grass, for she caught her breath and then let out a fierce oath, and this momentary delay lent Marie the respite to achieve the last twenty yards. But there was a fence between her and the road, and she knew that in the time it would take to climb the fence, Peter would reach her and haul her down.

To have come this far only to fail was more than she could bear. Her eyes misted with tears, and for an instant she did not see the man in the wagon, but heard him as he clicked his tongue to urge on his horse.

She clung to the fence to keep herself from falling, and tried to speak, but no sound came. The wheels grated and rumbled on the rough road. If she did not stop the man now he would be gone.

She waved her hand, and he saw her and raised his whip in greeting, but continued on his way. She waved again, attempting to express need and urgency in the movement of her arm, and he drew up. "Whoa! A good day to you. And what can I do for you?"

Marie found her voice. "Can you give me a ride into Rye?"

"Ay, that I can."

Peter put out her hand to pull Marie away, then hesitated and thought better of it.

Shakily Marie climbed the fence.

"I can take the both of you," the waggoner offered.

But Peter had turned and was walking back along the valley.

The man helped Marie up beside him, and looked at her curiously. "That man with you—" for he naturally took Peter to be a man, "—was he badgering you?"

"Yes," Marie replied, "he was badgering me."

"Ah! A nice young lady like you shouldn't be wandering alone through that valley. There's a house called Rippiers, and they don't say good things about it. Some foreign folk bought it a while back, and then they went away."

Marie had no desire to discuss Rippiers or the Vaudelets, and, finding she was not one for gossip, the man ceased talking and began to whistle instead.

When he had dropped her, Marie inquired as to where she might find the doctor, and went to his house. Fortunately he was at home and disengaged, and had his horse harnessed to his gig, and together he and Marie set out.

So different was the return journey that Marie's heart was light and her spirits rose. She chatted cheerfully to the doctor, and so short did the drive seem to be that she could scarcely believe it when they turned from the road into the park.

The doctor had asked for details of his patient, but Marie had been able to tell him little, merely that she had found him lying, bleeding and unconscious, having been shot.

"I reckon a gamekeeper was responsible," the doctor conjectured. "Those fellows are altogether too handy with the gun. Poaching is one thing but trespassing is another. People can stray on to private land without realising it. Heaven knows how many innocent trespassers have been picked off."

Marie was not anxious to discuss the matter further, for she was convinced that no one but Peter could have shot the man, and how could she explain Peter to the doctor, or, come to that, how explain Peter to anyone?

The doctor spent a considerable time with the wounded man, and when he came down Marie was waiting for him.

"Will he live?" she asked. It occurred to her that it was no concern of hers whether he lived or died. She wished him well only as one wishes any human being to recover from disaster.

"I have extracted the bullet, and the bleeding has almost ceased. He is young. Yes, I think it is most probable he will live. Tell me, the old woman, is she sensible and reliable?"

Marie hesitated. She wanted to say that Mrs Mumby would make a dependable nurse, because otherwise she feared the care of this man would devolve upon herself, and she had no wish to tend the stranger. But honesty forced her to answer, "I know little about her. She scarcely speaks. I think she is senile and feeble-minded."

"H'm!" The doctor looked closely at Marie. "And you, though strong-minded, are young."

"I am over seventeen," Marie told him, somewhat indignantly.

The doctor smiled. "But not much over. Well, the old woman seems anxious to nurse the boy, but keep an eye on her and on him, in case she should do something foolish."

Marie promised she would, but for several days was unable to enter the sick-room, for Mrs Mumby kept the door locked, both when she was within, and when she left, though this last was rarely, for the old man fetched and carried for her, mounting and descending the stairs a score of times a day.

Marie felt sorry for him. "You must be tired," she said. "Why don't you tell Mrs Mumby she must come down for some of the things she needs?"

Mr Mumby shook his head. "She won't leave him."

"Why not? He's out of danger now, isn't he?"

"She's an awkward woman when she's crossed."

"You are her husband. You must make her obey you," Marie said, with the unconscious arrogance of youth.

"Easier said than done, miss."

"But it must be done. Tell her she must rest and I will take her place."

"I don't think she would like that."

"Then she must dislike it." Marie spoke angrily. "I don't wish to be unkind, but you are servants and you must do as you are told."

The old man shook as if in terror, but he replied firmly and with courage. "Begging your pardon, miss, but we are not your servants."

"I am mistress here while Monsieur Alain is away."

"He's not our master neither."

"Then who is?"

The old man scratched his head, thinking. "Reckon it would be the old marquis, or if he's gone 'twould be Monsieur Rodolphe."

"They are all dead, the old marquis and Rodolphe and Gustave. There are only Monsieur Alain and I."

"You? You're nobody," Mr Mumby snapped.

Marie turned and walked away. It was beneath her dignity, she told herself, to discuss her legitimacy with the servants, but all the same she felt humiliated. When Alain came back, she resolved, she would tell him that the Mumbys had indeed outlived their usefulness, and she would urge him to retire them honourably and with an adequate pension.

Meanwhile there was the problem of controlling them in Alain's absence, and the crisis came when one morning Mr Mumby fell on the stairs dropping a tray of china. He was not seriously hurt, but was badly shaken and had twisted his ankle. Marie helped him down, and then ran up and knocked on the door of the sick-room.

"Mrs Mumby."

There was no sound from within. She knocked again, more loudly. "Mrs Mumby, I must speak to you."

The silence remained unbroken. "Mrs Mumby, if you do not unlock this door I shall send for someone to break it down." It was an empty threat. For whom could she send? Obviously Mrs Mumby was unmoved.

Marie played her last card. "Mrs Mumby, your husband has fallen down the stairs and hurt himself."

There was a rustling and shuffling and then the old woman spoke from the other side of the door. "Has he killed hisself?"

Marie was shocked by the calmness of Mrs Mumby's voice. "Of course not! But he has hurt his ankle, and all the china is broken."

He should take more care."

"Listen!" Marie spoke slowly and loudly, so that her words would penetrate. "Your husband has injured his ankle. He cannot walk, so there will be no food for you or your patient. There will be nothing to eat or drink. You will starve and so will he."

"You can bring it," the old woman said, indifferently. "You can leave it outside the door."

Marie was furious. "I shall do nothing of the kind. I shan't bring one crust of bread or a drink of water."

She heard Mrs Mumby spit. "Blasted young baggage! You darsn't let us lie here and rot."

"I dare. I swear that unless you let me into this room I will not come near you for a week."

She meant what she said, or at least in part, for she knew she must frighten the old woman into submission. The responsibility for the welfare of the wounded man was hers, for the doctor had not suggested coming again, and that Mrs Mumby was growing more eccentric, not to say mad, was evident. A day without food would kill neither nurse nor patient, and might serve to bring her to her senses.

But such a course was not necessary. Marie's voice must have carried conviction. There was the sound of the key turning, and the door was opened a few inches. Marie pushed it until it swung wide, and as she did so she was cold with the fear of what she might find.

SEVEN

The man was in bed, propped up by pillows, but at first Marie could see little of him, for Mrs Mumby scuttled across the room with unexpected speed and placed herself between Marie and the patient.

"Go away!" she shouted. "Go away!"

"I have as much right to be here as you have," Marie told her, reasonably. "Mr Mumby needs your attention."

"I can't leave him." She jerked her head towards the bed.

"I will stay."

"You won't hurt him?"

"Hurt him?" Marie echoed, in astonishment. "Why should I hurt him? We brought him here to be healed. I fetched the doctor, didn't I?"

Whether the old woman grasped what she was saying, Marie did not know, but when she pushed her aside Mrs Mumby did not resist, and after wavering irresolutely for a few moments, she left the room.

Though the man had as yet said nothing, he was fully conscious, watching, and Marie's first impression was surprise at his youth. He could not be more than two or three years older than herself. His face was pale, perhaps due to the loss of blood, and he had a shock of dark, unruly hair. There were bandages around and over his left shoulder, and his arm was in a sling.

Marie said, politely, "I trust you are feeling better."

To her amazement there was no conventional response. He glared at her. "Didn't manage to kill me this time, did you?

Got me in the back of my shoulder. A few inches lower and it would have gone through my heart."

"What are you talking about? Why should I want to shoot you?"

"You know best." He closed his eyes, as if to convey to her that the conversation held no further interest.

"I don't know. I don't know anything about it. I think you must be mad, or delirious. I've never seen you before in my life. As for shooting, I would be afraid to hold a gun in my hand."

"Didn't have to hold it, did you?" His eyes opened wide.

"What do you mean?"

"Oh, stop playing the innocent!" he exclaimed, angrily.

"I am innocent, and you are talking nonsense. You were shot, so someone had to fire a gun."

"Why do you have to pretend? You know very well that you rigged up a spring-gun and a trip-wire."

"I have no idea what those things are."

"The Vaudelets always used them, spring-guns and man-traps and gin-traps. It started when the oldest marquis came from France during the Revolution. He was afeared the people as they called the sans-culottes would be after him. From then it became the custom and it was the gamekeeper's job to set 'em up."

Marie nodded, remembering the waggoner. "No wonder people don't say good things about Rippiers."

"At least it kept poachers away. But it killed my father. He got careless and tripped over one of his own wires. Now I fell for the same trick."

"I think it is cruel and wicked," Marie declared, heatedly. "All traps should be forbidden, whether to catch men or beasts, and to imagine I could set such a snare—well, that's ridiculous. If you want to know the truth, it was done by someone called Peter."

"Peter? Peter wouldn't do it. Peter is my friend."

"Oh, no!" She wanted to tell him that Peter was a strange, warped being, friend to no-one, but only the whole complicated story could explain, and so she contented herself with saying, "Peter is a woman."

"I know that. She's living in my house."

For a few minutes Marie could think of nothing to say. This man acknowledged Peter as his friend, which meant— What did it mean?

"Peter laid that trap," she insisted, "but it was intended for me, not for you."

He laughed. "You are a fool."

"All right. I may be a fool, but that supposes I am no villain, and if I am not responsible there is no one who could have done it except Peter. Do you imagine poor old Mr or Mrs Mumby wish to murder either of us?"

"No. It wouldn't be them." For the first time he appeared to be giving some consideration to what she was saying. "Why would Peter wish to kill you?"

"She tried before. I thought, then, after my aunt died, that it was because she wanted the tavern for herself. But now— It might have something to do with my mother's letter."

"None of that makes sense to me," the young man said, crossly.

"Sometime I will tell you about it." She realised she was being imprudent, and added, "But I don't think you would be interested. What is your name?"

"Jenkin Sparks."

"I am Marie Vaudelet."

"That's a lie!"

"How dare you say such a thing!" She was so angry that she threw caution overboard. "My mother was legally married to Monsieur Rodolphe. It is in her letter, and also it is written that he left her the treasure."

"Treasure? What do you know about the treasure?"

She realised she had been stupid to mention this. "Why, nothing. I know nothing except that the treasure should belong to me. If there is a treasure."

"Oh, yes! There's a treasure. My father used to tell me about it. It was the talk of the estate, in the days when there were servants and tenants. The oldest marquis managed to smuggle it out of France when he escaped. It was gold and jewels. One or two of the gems came from the French crown jewels, or so they say."

Marie was entranced. This was like a fairy-tale. "What happened to it?"

"The oldest marquis hid it, and seems he didn't tell his son where he put it. Leastways, they never took it with them when they returned to France."

"Then how did they live?"

"Reckon they got back the money and estates they left when they came away. Why wouldn't they? Revolutions all end the same. The rich stay rich and the poor stay poor."

"I don't see—" Marie began, and then stopped. Perhaps at last she was beginning to see. If there really were a treasure, and this man believed she had a clue to its whereabouts, then she was in greater danger than she had even imagined. How much had Peter told him? Had she confided in him, possibly shown him the letter? Was it pretence on his part when he declared he knew nothing of it?

She determined to have as little as possible to do with Jenkin, but Mrs Mumby, now that she had decided Marie threatened no harm to her patient, became less possessive, and was ready enough to leave her in charge of the sickroom.

"It's my feet," Mrs Mumby complained. "They can't manage them stairs, and what with Mr Mumby and his ankle—well, it's like we're getting too old for some things."

Marie was becoming little more than a servant, she found. To get the Mumbys to obey an order of hers was wellnigh impossible. Fervently she looked forward to Alain's return. He had been gone longer than he had calculated, for it was two months since his departure.

It was not long before Jenkin was able to leave his bed, and Marie was relieved of the task of waiting on him, though to her surprise she found she missed his company, hostile though he was, dangerous though she believed him to be.

He took his meals with the Mumbys, and Marie saw him

rarely, yet she believed he roamed the house, soft-footed and secret, for frequently she had the feeling that she was being watched.

She thought, I am becoming overwrought, hysterical, imagining persecution where there is none. But one day when she was in the library, taking down some of the old books, dusting them and opening them to the air, she heard a sound and went quickly to the door and flung it wide, and there was Jenkin, pressed so closely to it that he almost fell into the room.

"What are you doing?" she demanded.

"I was passing."

"Do you pass with your eye to the keyhole?"

He denied it. "I was not spying." But he spoke so unconcernedly that it was as if he did not care what she thought.

"Isn't it time you went home?" she asked. "Your shoulder is almost healed."

"I've got no home."

"What of your house in the woods?"

"That's a hovel."

"Only because you've made it so," she told him, severely. "What of those poor dead animals and birds, hung up like washing on a line? I don't know how you can be so cruel."

"My father caught them. People reckoned he was the best trapper in Sussex. But I didn't enjoy killing. He said I had a weak stomach."

"Then why don't you take down the skins and the skeletons, now your father is dead?"

"Well, 'tis not so long since he died, and I guess I'm so used to the varmints that I don't notice 'em any more."

"Well, you can go and clear them all away."

"I like it here."

Marie drew herself up. She had allowed the Mumbys to get out of hand, but now she must assert herself. Certainly she would not be browbeaten by an unpleasant youth like Jenkin.

"You may like it here, but you cannot stay indefinitely. You have no position in the house."

"Position? What do I want with position? I can help the two old ones. Lord knows they need help."

"You are a gamekeeper. Your work is on the estate."

"What work?" he asked, mockingly. "What estate? There's no game to keep."

"There's other work to be done besides protecting one kind of bird and killing others. Why don't you rid the woods of all the rotten stuff so that the trees have room to breathe?"

"Is those your orders, mistress?"

"Yes."

"Well, you're not my mistress, and I can't be sacked 'cos I never was employed. The Vaudelets left here before I was born. As far as they know, I don't exist."

"Then you don't get paid?"

He shrugged his shoulders. "It doesn't bother me."

"But how do you live?"

"I manage. I don't enjoy killing, but when my stomach's empty enough I can snare a rabbit or a pheasant. Besides, I come down here most once a week and the old woman gives me bread and suchlike."

"She has no right to do that."

"Why not? It's out of her wages. You don't suppose there's money sent for food or for keeping up the house, do you?"

"I don't know, but I shall speak to Alain—to Monsieur Vaudelet. Everything will be settled and put right when he returns. So go back to your hut, and when your shoulder is well you can do something useful."

"I shall go when I please and where I please, Miss High-and-Mighty."

Marie could have wept from frustration and helplessness. How did one exert authority, she wondered, in the face of open defiance?

"What about Peter?" she asked. "She won't know what has happened to you."

"She?" He laughed. "She'll not care. She's not my whore,

you know. She's twice my age, and she's grown to be half a man. She just stays with me because it suits her, and I let her stay because she knows a way to make us both rich."

"What is that?"

"Never you mind!"

An idea occurred to Marie. What better way to aid her own safety than to sow dissention between these two conspirators? Besides, unfriendly though he was, Jenkin deserved better than to fall under the influence of one as wicked as Peter.

"When you get back," she said, "you had better tell Peter that her plot misfired. I'm sure she didn't intend *you* to be shot."

"She didn't do it."

"Then who did? You can't still believe that I set that gun. If I had wanted you to die, I could have left you lying there, but I didn't. I helped carry you into the house, then went to fetch a doctor. Surely you have sense enough to see that I couldn't be the person who tried to kill you."

From his expression it was obvious that her words had at last sunk in. He was puzzled, and he had begun to doubt his own interpretation of what had happened, but it did not appear to change his attitude towards Marie. He went away without a word, and Marie did not see him about the house.

She asked the Mumbys what had happened to Jenkin, but they did not consider the question worth answering, for they pretended the deafness which came so easily to them.

The loneliness was hard to bear, and Marie reflected wryly that, lacking a friend, an enemy could be better than no one at all.

EIGHT

After Jenkin had gone Marie made no attempt to return to her former habit of visitng the stables. The sight of Peter in the harness room, and the finding of Jenkin by the stream had invested those places with a kind of horror. The trap of a spring-gun having been placed once among the trees, was there not the possibility it might be set there again? There was nowhere she could go in safety. So she dressed herself in her fine new clothes, and sat at the window of the small study, reflecting that now she was indeed like a princess in a tower, favoured with everything but freedom.

So often had the unexpected happened to her that she might have guessed there would soon be a change. She sat at her window, one evening, and so lulled was she by the quietness that the sound of hooves and wheels made her start up in a fright.

She went to the door and opened it slightly, then paused. Here was her sanctuary and she was reluctant to leave it, but even as she hesitated she heard in the distance the sound of voices, and one there was no mistaking.

She flew down the stairs. "Alain! Oh, Alain, you have come home!"

He stood in the hall, surrounded by a mountain of luggage, and two or three men were running back and forth, bringing in more boxes. When he saw Marie he held out both hands, and she ran and clasped them.

"Marie! How wonderful you look! I declare there has been a wand waved over you which has transformed you into the most beautiful lady."

She was laughing as she had not laughed for weeks.

"Don't tell me you have brought all this stuff in one carriage!"

"Indeed, no! I sent it on by the railway from London. It was awaiting me at Rye, and I needed three conveyances to cart it. But this is nothing. There is furniture to follow, and tomorrow workmen will arrive to commence the restoration of the house."

"Oh, Alain!" She felt she could for ever continue exclaiming, "Oh, Alain!" She found her hands were still in his, and she drew them gently away, saying, shyly, "I am so glad to see you."

"I am glad also to see you," he said, but whether he spoke from politeness or from the heart she did not know.

She thought of the Mumbys, and of the many things she had to tell him. "May I speak to you, alone?"

"Of course! As soon as this lumber is cleared away."

But it was not until the following morning that she was able to get him by himself, and even then it was nearing midday, for she had been up for hours when he appeared.

"I rarely rise before noon," he told her, as if in answer to an unspoken question. "The day is so long. I declare the sun himself must be weary before he sets."

"The days have been long since I have been here,"she confessed.

"Why? Do you not like the country?"

"No, it's not that." She spoke quickly, feeling he must think her ungrateful. "It's because I have been rather lonely without you. After all, the Mumbys are rather old."

"Yes, they are old and useless, and they are servants, not fit companions for you."

"Well, they are not really useless." She wanted to be fair to them. "Alain, you won't turn them out, will you?"

He shrugged his shoulders. "I had not thought about it, but I doubt whether my new chef will allow such a hag in his kitchen."

"Oh, but what will happen?" She was alarmed for them.

"Mr Mumby is terrified they might have to go to the workhouse."

"Which could be the best place for them."

"Alain, you couldn't be so cruel!"

"My dearest cousin, you sound so fierce, and you look so dignified in that delightful morning dress that I am half afraid of you. How could I bear to have you think me cruel?"

"Then you will retain them?"

"They must retire, but I can give them a pension, and I dare say some place can be found for them. Rippiers is large."

"I knew you would be kind," Marie said, happily. "You have been so good to me. I have not yet thanked you for the beautiful clothes. Miss Grey is very clever."

"She has provided you with everything you need?"

"Everything and more. I never dreamed I would possess such lovely things." She frowned. "Alain, what is to become of me?"

"What do you mean?"

"Well, unless proof of my mother's marriage can be found, I have no right to anything belonging to the Vaudelet family. This is your house. I cannot live here for ever on your charity."

"You must not think of it as charity."

"To me it is, and soon I must go away, find work to do. I've not been trained for anything, but they say everybody has one talent or another. I've read many books since I've been here, and from Mr Cooperthwayte I learned Latin and Greek and French. Perhaps I could teach."

Alain laid his hands over hers. "You must not think of it. At least, not yet. In any case, I do not approve of ladies working."

"I am not a lady, Alain, not a real one. Whatever happened to my mother, it's true she was a servant."

"To me, Marie, you are a real lady. Doesn't that count with you?"

"Oh, yes! But—" She hesitated. There was so much to tell

him, and it was only fair that he should know everything. "—but it may not be wise for me to stay here. It may cause trouble for you. It is Peter."

Carefully, meticulously, Marie told him the whole story of what had happened during his absence, leaving out nothing. "She means to try to kill me. I can't think why, for I have done her no harm. When you took me away, she was left with the tavern and all the money you gave her. I imagined she would be content. Why should she follow me? Oh, Alain, I have been so dreadfully afraid, but now you are here I feel safe."

Alain looked troubled, even nervous, and Marie was touched that he should be concerned for her. "Truly I am no longer frightened," she assured him. "Now you have come home the house is smiling."

Alain's expression did not change. Clearly he was taking seriously the threat of Peter. "It is possible," he said, slowly, "that she intends me as her victim."

"How could she?" Marie asked, puzzled. "She has received nothing but benefit from you."

"How can we assess the working of the mind of such a creature? But we must protect ourselves. Fortunately the men I brought with me are stout fellows. I shall arm them with guns, and they will take turn to do sentry duty, day and night."

A sense of security descended on Marie. "It will be like living in a fortress," she said, lightly, as if she spoke of a game.

But to Alain it was not play. "A fortress is what I shall make of the house," and his voice was grim.

She thought she would not mind being shut up in this place, with Alain as protector, but in the weeks that followed there was no question of confinement. Masons and carpenters swarmed everywhere. The great doors were propped open to receive the pieces of furniture that arrived. The sounds of sawing and hammering were as hopeful and reassuring as if they heralded the recovery of Rippiers from a wasting disease.

Once more there were horses in the stables, and Alain insisted on teaching Marie to ride. She was quick to learn and had no fear of the animals, but when she had progressed sufficiently to be able to venture further afield, she began to show signs of nervousness.

"I don't—I don't care to go too far from the house."

She thought he might laugh at her, but he understood.

"You will be safe with me, dear cousin. I carry a pistol, never go out without it. That woman would think twice before attacking us."

During August he took the trouble to rise early, that they might ride in the freshness of the morning, before the heat of the day, and Marie knew that never before in her life had she been so happy. After her lonely childhood it was a delight to have a constant companion, one to whom she could talk without reserve, one to whom she could listen with profit and pleasure as he spoke of his experiences both in England and France, of his acquaintanceship with the cultured and the famous. So much she dreaded he might go away again that she dared not ask if such a thing were likely.

One morning Alain suggested, "Let us go to that hut in the woods."

She tried to think of a refusal which would neither offend nor disappoint him. "There is nothing to see. It's a miserable place."

"All the same, we should inspect it. We've not had a glimpse of that woman Peter. She may have left the district. In which case we can relax our vigilance."

Marie made the only excuse she could think of. "I'm not sure I could find it again."

"Then we shall search until we do." He spoke gaily, as if anxious for the adventure.

There was nothing more she could say, and side by side they rode up the slope to the dark line of the woods. As they went between the close-set trees the sun vanished as suddenly as if it had been snuffed out, and Marie shivered.

"It is cold here," she explained, but she knew that this was not the reason for the chill she felt.

Almost she hoped she would be unable to find the clearing, for then it would be as if it did not exist; yet to find it quickly would be preferable, otherwise they might ride around for hours.

There was no landmark she remembered, and she was astonished when after a very short time they came upon the open glade. Had it not been for the hut she would not have recognised the place. Gone were the lines with their string of gruesome exhibits, gone were the poles upholding them. There was even a certain neatness about the clearing, for the nettles and brambles and some of the rougher grass had been scythed down and lay in swathes, dried to the consistency of hay.

Alain dismounted. "I will see if anyone is at home. Are you coming?"

She shook her head and watched him knocking on the door and then peering through the window, as she had done. She was uneasy, and the fact that no one was about did nothing to allay her disquiet. She glanced from side to side, fearful for Alain and for herself, and she was relieved when, after what seemed much longer than a few minutes, he crossed the clearing and came back to her.

"I think our friend has departed."

"Jenkin Sparks is still here."

"Well, I suppose he has a certain right to be."

"Peter is here as well."

Alain looked surprised. "Have you seen her?"

"No."

"Then how—"

"Let us go!" she urged. "Please, Alain, let us go now, at once!"

He glanced at her inquiringly, but she could not explain, had no way of telling him why she knew that Peter was still haunting these woods. It was simply a sensation of corruption, a smell of evil.

NINE

As they rode back from the hut in the woods Alain said little and appeared deep in thought, and when Marie had made several abortive attempts at conversation she decided it would be more considerate to respect his mood.

She expected he would have regained his good spirits by the time they dined, but his absent-mindedness persisted, and she became troubled on his account. "Is anything wrong, Alain?"

His head jerked up, as though he had been startled out of a dream. "What? No, of course there is nothing wrong. Why should there be?"

Her answer came in the form of a question. "Do you think Peter has gone away? I could feel her all around, when we were in the woods."

"That was imagination."

"She frightens me."

"Don't worry. You are protected now."

Her heart swelled with gratitude. "You are so good to me. But what have I done to make Peter my enemy? She already has my mother's letter."

"What could she want with the letter?"

"Perhaps she thinks it may help her to find the treasure."

"But apparently my great-grandfather did not tell my grandfather of the treasure. My father knew nothing about it. How was my uncle able to speak of it to your mother?"

"I thought about that, and I reckoned that the oldest marquis told my father—your uncle—because he was eldest grandson."

"Why did he not tell my grandfather, his son?"

"Perhaps he didn't like him very much," Marie said, naïvely.

Alain laughed. "After all you are a practical young lady. But you have broken a promise you made to me."

"I have?" She knitted her brows. "Oh, I'm sure I can't have done. If I promised—I could never break a promise I made to you. What was it?"

"You promised to write down your mother's letter."

"Oh, that!" She was relieved. It seemed such a small thing. "I will do it. Of course I will!"

"Then why not today? It would be sad if you were to forget it, and we may never retrieve it from Peter. You will want to keep it for the rest of your life."

She thanked him for reminding her. How sensible he was! Sure as she had been that she would never forget the letter, there was the possibility that when she grew old, as old as the Mumbys, her mind would become as confused as theirs.

As soon as they had finished dinner, she went to the library where, on a small table near a window, were the writing materials she required, and she sat down happily, convinced this was a task which would be completed in a short time.

"My Dearest Sister," she wrote.

"Though we have been estranged, I write to ask of you a favour—" But was it necessary to record her mother's apologies and regrets? Was it even right? What her mother had done she had done for the sake of love, and for that had paid dearly, as her daughter had later paid in poverty and loneliness.

In her mind the letter continued. "—to live in a house such as Rippiers, even as a servant—" Yes, and what next? "I loved Rodolphe so much—"

She wrote down a few sentences, and then found she could not quite remember the wording of what followed. Did it matter? The incidents were clear to her, the secret wedding in Paris, the plans of the Vaudelets to arrange for Rodolphe an advantageous match, the anguish of the young couple, and then Rodolphe's fatal illness. The facts might be sufficient for Marie, but would they be enough for Alain?

She racked her brains as stray sentences came to her. "—they were all very angry with me. ... They'll not treat you well, but remember the treasure ... he could scarcely speak, but he beckoned me closer—"

Then he had whispered something. Marie could almost remember it. It was on the tip of her tongue, as they say. It was a number, and then another word. Well, it was probably not important.

The next paragraph had impressed itself more firmly on her mind in its pathos and injustice. "Gustave and Gustave's wife would not allow me to attend the funeral. ... The marquis commanded me to leave the house. ... I was with child, and I was afraid of what they might do to me."

Yes, she could write all that down, but would it not cause pain to Alain to learn of the inhumanity of his parents? They had acted cold-bloodedly, without pity, condemning to destitution, and perhaps death, their brother's wife and child; but all that was in the past, when Alain had been a young, innocent boy.

She sighed, put down her pen and tore up the paper on which she had written the disjointed sentences. Alain might think her foolish, a flitter-brained female who could not hold a memory for more than a month or two, and in part he would be right. She had believed that every word of her mother's letter was written indelibly on her mind, and she could only suppose it was the fear and excitement and utter transformation of her recent life which had caused her partially to forget.

She went outside, to the small garden beneath the study window, and seated herself beside the pool, dabbling her hand in the water, and there Alain found her.

"Where is the letter?" he asked immediately.

"I'm sorry, Alain. I couldn't remember much of it."

"You couldn't remember?" He sounded thunderstruck.

"I'll never forget the meaning of it, and I remember odd sentences, but I couldn't put the whole thing together."

"You said you recalled every word."

"Well, I do, in a way. I remember *what* my mother said, but not *how* she said it."

"You little fool!" She had not seen him as angry as this. He stood beside her, towering over her, and for a moment she was afraid of him. But then she thought of his kindness, his generosity, and she realised she was to blame. Of course he was disappointed! Unintentionally she had misled him.

"I didn't realise," she confessed. "I didn't realise it was possible for me to forget something so important. But so much has been happening that things from the past are going out of my head."

"You told me you had the letter by heart. Otherwise I would have forced the woman to give it to me."

Dolefully she pulled at the blades of grass around her. "Can't you make her do so now?"

"Where can we find her? She has vanished into thin air."

"Jenkin Sparks may know where she is."

"It would appear he is equally elusive."

"I think Mrs Mumby could find him. She nursed him after he was shot and she seems—" Marie hesitated. What, if anything, was between the boy and the old woman she did not know. "—she seems to care for him," she finished.

Gently Alain lowered himself on to the ground beside her.

"I'm sorry I was angry with you," he apologised. "Perhaps you don't realise how important it is that we should find Great-grandfather's treasure."

"Oh, I know it is." She clasped her hands together. "If only my mother had defied your parents, if after they turned her from the house she had gone to the law for protection—"

"We are not concerned with such incidents," he broke in, coldly. "They are in the past."

She was bewildered. "But we are speaking of the past, are we not? My mother's letter—"

Again he lost his temper. "The complaints of a servant girl

against her employers are not important. If my parents turned her out, they no doubt had good reason for doing so."

Marie sprang to her feet. "How dare you!" she cried. "How dare you speak ill of my mother! Of what do you accuse her? Of loving my father? Of marrying him? If we are going to abuse with hard words, what couldn't I say of your parents? That my mother went in fear of her life? That she was afraid they might murder her and her unborn child? Oh, you're a fine one to talk, Alain Vaudelet!"

"Be quiet, Marie! Give me a chance to explain. I said nothing that—"

"You've said everything against my mother. You despise her because she was poor and humble. Well, I despise your parents because they were greedy and unscrupulous."

"We do no good by inveighing against the dead," Alain told her, wearily. "Come, sit down, and let us talk reasonably."

Marie ignored this. "Why should you wish to know what was in my mother's letter? You're not interested in the misery she suffered. You want to hear about the treasure, that's all. But I shall not tell you. The treasure, if we found it, would be mine, for my father on his death-bed promised it to my mother."

"You have no witness to that. If my parents heard him, they are not alive to testify."

"You are a wealthy man," Marie declared, scornfully. "Aren't you content? Do you hanker after more?"

"Stay! Let me finish! If we should find the treasure, you are welcome to it."

"I want nothing that's not mine by right. I want my mother's name cleared. I want it proved that she was my father's legal wife."

"You are too ambitious. You want the moon."

"Perhaps I do, but I will not tell you what was in my mother's letter."

"That is a childish trick," he said, contemptuously. "We

both know that you have forgotten. Why can't you trust me, Marie? Haven't I given you everything you wanted?"

She looked down at the dress she was wearing, at the fine white muslin sprigged with tiny clusters of forget-me-nots, at the lace and ribbons which trembled beneath her anger as if fluttering in a breeze. "Oh, yes! You have given me every-thing. But I will not have you fling me the treasure like a trinket, as you gave me the bed I sleep in and the clothes I am wearing. I hate you, Alain Vaudelet!" And she turned and ran, stumbling and almost falling because of the tears that blinded her.

TEN

Fume at her helplessness though she might, there was no escaping the facts. Marie depended on Alain for the food she ate and the clothes she wore. The least she could do in return would be to make herself amenable to his wishes, obey his orders. Now, she supposed, she should apologise for her behaviour and straightaway write down whatever she remembered from her mother's letter. Yet somehow she was reluctant to do either of these things. Alain's attitude towards family matters had been strangely inconsistent. He had told her she would be welcome to any treasure she might find, but he had been extremely angry that she could not remember her mother's reference to the treasure.

So the barrier between them remained unbroken, and what had seemed to be a growing companionship now languished. Politely they met at meals, and ate in near silence. Politely they went their different ways, and for Marie Rippiers again became a lonely place.

Frequently she contemplated begging Alain's forgiveness, ignoring her conviction that he was as much to blame as she was for the estrangement. Surely anything was better than such a miserable state of affairs, particularly as she felt his unhappiness to be equal to hers. But she did not succeed in carrying out her intention. Something always held her back at the last moment.

So the weeks passed, as summer dipped into autumn, and Marie began to feel they might stay like this for ever.

It was all the more unexpected, even startling, when one morning Alain made an announcement.

He said, "My sister is coming from France."

Surprise and interest and pleasure swept through Marie. So little had he spoken about his sister that Marie had almost forgotten her existence.

"Oh, that's wonderful! When will she arrive?"

"Within a few days."

There were a thousand questions she wanted to ask, but she did not know where to begin.

She contented herself, therefore, with, "What is her name?"

"Blanche."

"Just Blanche?"

"She has some other names, as you have, but they are not important." He spoke coolly, as though to discourage further questions.

But Marie persisted. "How old is she?"

"Four years younger than I am."

"Ah, that is better!" As Marie said it she realised it sounded impolite, and added, hastily, "I mean, she is nearer my age. She won't be too old for me." Oh dear! she thought, this is going from bad to worse. Why must I give a bad impression, when really I would like to please him? She made a further amendment. "Not that you are old."

She put a light shawl about her shoulders, for though the sun was shining the wind had a touch of chill, and she went from the house to walk a short distance through the park. She was deep in thought, wondering whether Blanche's visit would make any difference, either for good or ill: wondering whether it was for a brief visit Blanche was coming, or whether it was to take up residence.

So much wondering did Marie do that when she looked up she found she had walked further than she had intended. She had climbed the hill, as she liked to do, for it gave a splendid view of the house, but today she had reached the first scattered trees on the edge of the woods. Her nervousness was not as acute as it had been. The presence of servants and stablemen and gardeners had removed much of the threatening atmosphere. From where she stood she could see a gardener working among the vegetables, and a stableboy exercising one of the horses, and the sight was reassuring. It was a relief to feel herself calm and brave.

She sensed, rather than heard, someone behind her, and swung round. Jenkin was there, standing motionless, and the sudden shock made her angry. "What are you doing here?"

"No harm," he replied, mildly.

"You gave me a start."

"Footsteps don't sound on grass"

Her instinct was to run from him, but she restrained it.

"You tidied up the clearing," she said, "and took down the dead birds and animals."

"How do you know?"

"I rode up there with Alain. He wanted to see Peter."

"Ah, I reckon he would."

"What do you mean by that?"

Jenkin smiled. "You and me, we must talk different languages, 'cos we never properly understand one another, do we?"

"That," Marie explained, "is because you are keeping things back, and probably I am as well. We don't trust each other."

"I don't trust nobody."

"I don't know much about you, and you don't know anything about me."

"I know you talk like a lady, except sometimes, when you forget. But underneath you're just ordinary, like me. And you're right pretty. My father told me never to trust a pretty woman."

"Why not?"

"Because prettiness don't last, and so pretty women have got to feather their nests and look out for number one."

"Your father didn't know much about women."

"He knew about one woman, my mother. She left us when I was a little baby, and went off with another man."

"I'm sorry." It sounded an inadequate comment, but she

could think of nothing else to say. She turned, as if to move away, but Jenkin caught her by the upper arm and swung her round. So roughly did he do this that she was frightened.

"Don't go!" he commanded. "I haven't finished."

"I can't wait. I shall be late."

"Why are you afraid of me?"

"I didn't say I was."

"Why?" he insisted.

"Well, you said Peter was your friend, and Peter wants to kill me."

"What makes you think that?"

"She hunts me as if I were a wild animal. I've been afraid to go out alone."

"She might want you alive, not dead."

"When she set the spring-gun? That was intended for me, not you. You don't know her like I do. Back in Wapping she locked me in the cellar and then kept me for months a prisoner in my own room."

"But she didn't murder you."

"Peter is a criminal."

"Aren't we all?" Jenkin asked. "Is there anybody as knows all the laws that have been made? Gamekeeper. Poacher. Where's the difference, except the gamekeeper can take what he wants in broad daylight?"

"When Peter was a servant she murdered her mistress."

"But if the master or mistress murdered the servant it wouldn't be the same, would it? They'd do it in self-defence and call the servant a trespasser or a robber."

"Peter wanted the Leather Bottle for herself, after Aunt died. And then she read my mother's letter and thought she'd get more if I led her to the treasure, so she found where the de Vaudelets lived, and sent for Alain."

"I know. She told me."

Marie sighed. "It's so stupid, chasing me around. Why doesn't she come to the house and talk sensibly?"

"And be arrested, and then transported or hanged?"

"I wouldn't—"

"Maybe not. But Monsieur Vaudelet would. Anyway, you're too late. Peter's dead."

"Dead?" Marie thought she had misheard.

"Yes. You've nothing more to fear. I found her. She'd been shot."

"But who—"

"You may well ask," Jenkin said, fiercely. "Who would want to be rid of her? Who provided his servants with guns?"

It was difficult to credit what she had been told. For so long Peter had been a menace to her that Marie could scarcely believe that menace had been removed. She was torn between relief and a feeling that such a relief was unworthy. One should not rejoice at a death, even the death of such a person as Peter.

Her immediate response was to defend Alain. "Monsieur Vaudelet would never do a thing like that, or order his servants to do so."

"Oh, no!" Jenkin exclaimed sardonically. "Gentlemen don't, do they? That's why they are gentlemen."

"What did you do when you found her?"

"Buried her, of course."

"After you reported the crime?"

"Reported?" Jenkin stared at her as if he thought her mad. "Why would I report it?"

"It's the proper thing to do. It's the law."

"And what would happen? The police would come sneaking around, and before you could say knife they'd be blaming me. I've no wish for a necklace of hemp."

"Someone will find out."

"Who? Who will miss Peter? She's been dead to the world for years."

Suddenly Marie remembered an important item, perhaps the most important aspect of Peter's death. "He'll want the letter, my mother's letter."

"D'you want him to have it?"

Marie hesitated. Her first impulse was to say, "Of course I

do!" Wasn't it the obvious, the sensible reply? If the treasure were to be found, it would be necessary for Alain to help her. What would be gained by keeping the letter selfishly to herself?

She prevaricated by saying, "He'll come looking for it."

Jenkin winked. "He won't find it. I've got it hidden in a safe place."

"You've no right to it," Marie said, angrily. "It is from my mother and it belongs to me. You must give it to me."

"What would happen if I did? You'd take it straight to his lordship."

"What I do with it is my business."

"Yes, and that's why I'm going to hang on to it."

"If I tell Alain, he'll soon get it from you."

"Reckon he would. Reckon I'd meet with an accident, same as Peter did."

"Why is everyone so stupid?" she raged. "Why do they do such foolish, wicked things for my mother's simple letter?" She looked up as she spoke, as though demanding an answer from heaven, and there in the sky was a globe, ghostly as a daylight moon, but moving more swiftly than any moon would do. For a moment she was awed, as though at a miraculous vision, and then she saw it for what it was.

"Gracious!" she cried. "Look at that balloon!"

ELEVEN

They stared, and their wonder was almost as great as if this manifestation had indeed been an answer from heaven. Jenkin had never seen a balloon before, and Marie had no more than caught a glimpse of Mr James Glaisher's as he had ascended over London just before sunset two years previously."

" 'Tis beautiful," Jenkin said, reverently.

But Marie thought of the man or men risking their lives for something of no conceivable practical purpose. "If we were intended to fly we'd be given wings," she said, crossly, and deliberately turned her attention from the globe which suddenly flashed a golden light as it caught the sun.

"My mother's letter cannot be of interest to you."

Jenkin did not reply. At that moment nothing existed for him except the balloon. The schemes of men seemed small and nasty compared with the shining vessel in the sky.

Marie saw the uselessness of further discussion. "I must go home," she said, and ran down the hillside.

When she reached the drive in front of the house she found the servants grouped there, watching the balloon. One of them said, "She is drifting."

"Ay," another agreed. "Breeze is freshening. No knowing where she'll come down now."

Annoyed at what she looked upon as their impertinence at ignoring her arrival, Marie asked, tartly, "Have you never seen a balloon before?"

They shook their heads. "No, miss."

"Well, now you have seen it and it is almost out of sight, so don't you think you should get on with your work?"

So used were they to receiving orders that they began to move away, but an under-footman, noted for being a cheeky boy, answered her back. "Us be troubled for master, even if you bain't."

"Wait a minute!" she commanded, sharply. "What do you mean? What about your master?"

"Why, up there."

"Up there?" A quivering weakness ran through her. "Don't tell me Monsieur Vaudelet is—is in that balloon!"

"He is, right enough. We helped him when he inflated it, and then we held the ropes until he was ready to take off, and we—" The boy gave these details, appearing to think she required proof of Alain's involvement.

"Why?" Marie interrupted. "Why should he do such a thing? Does he know anything about ballooning?"

"Oh, yes! Says he went up often when he was in France. He brought the balloon with him. In a crate it was. You'd never think it would fold so small."

Her anxiety lost its edge, but still she saw this as a crisis. The sky was a dangerous place, a place of accidents. Already a number of aeronauts had lost their lives.

She turned to the stableboy. "Saddle three horses."

"Three?"

"Yes, one for me and one for you and one for the master. The wind is blowing the balloon inland. We must follow it."

The boy stared at her, open-mouthed. "On horseback?"

"How else? Hurry now!"

The boy did not require any further persuasion. This, in his opinion, was a rare adventure.

They rode off at a smart trot, the boy leading the spare horse. By now the balloon was out of sight, and Marie asked, "Is the wind from the south?"

"No, miss. South-west I should reckon."

"Well, I don't know these parts. Which road must we take?"

The boy was nervous, reluctant to accept responsibility. It was always easy to blame the servants.

Marie knew what he was thinking.

She told the boy, "I shall say I chose the way to go. Whatever happens that's what I shall say."

He cast her a glance of gratitude. "We'd best take the road to Ashford, and if we don't catch the balloon before then, we'll carry on towards Canterbury." Even as he spoke he thought the words sounded mad and fantastic. Catch the balloon? As well try to catch a falling star.

They rode at a good pace, and whenever they were clear of trees and hedgerows they looked for the balloon. The early brightness and clearness of the day was disappearing, for clouds had come up with the wind, and Marie had a feeling it would rain before evening.

"Balloons can rise above the clouds," she said, "so it could be quite near without being in sight."

"Well, we'll have to rest the horses before long."

They slowed to a walk, disheartened. Soon, if they had no success, they must think of returning to Rippiers, if they hoped to reach it before night. There was no question of staying out, or even having a meal, for Marie had no money with her.

At that moment when despondency was sinking almost to despair she looked up, and there, to the left of them, was the balloon. It was a couple of miles away, and was little more than the height of the tallest trees. From its car a rope dangled, trailing behind it as it drifted sluggishly along.

"Come!" she cried, urging her horse forward. "We must go straight towards it. Open the gate!"

The boy looked shocked. "Not that one! 'Tis a cornfield not yet cut."

"What does it matter?"

"Farmer will think it matters."

"The balloon might have come down in it. Monsieur Vaudelet will compensate him."

"Money don't make up for losing corn. Please, miss! Look,

there's a lane running alongside, just down there. We'll waste no time. It'll be quicker, in fact."

She allowed herself to be persuaded, and they trotted briskly down the lane and cantered across a pasture. The balloon had by now dipped down behind a small hill, and as they approached this they heard voices, the loudest of which was Alain's. No words were audible, but as soon as they had breasted the hill it was obvious what was happening. Alain had thrown out several ropes as well as the guide-rope, and was instructing two men to catch hold of them, but the men, farmers or farm-labourers, had evidently never seen a balloon before, and, having it descend upon them without warning, were frightened out of their wits.

"Come on!" Alain yelled. "Stir yourselves, you blockheads! Grab a rope! It won't bite you."

The balloon bumped against the ground and bounced off to about twenty feet in the air.

"You half-witted clods! Run, damn you!"

Marie urged her horse to a gallop. "Loose the leading rein!" she cried to the boy, realising that the spare horse would slow him down, and together they plunged down the incline. The men, jolted into activity by the sight of something as normal and of this world as horses and riders, began to run behind them.

At the bottom of the field was a wood. The balloon brushed against a stout oak-tree, wobbled, and descended sufficiently for Marie to take hold of the end of a rope, while the boy did likewise. They felt as though their arms would be pulled from their sockets, but here in the shelter of the trees there was little or no wind. The balloon settled, Alain was able to jump from the car, and the two men arrived to lend their assistance. In a few minutes the monster was secured, Alain opened the valve, and quickly the great gilded globe sagged and lost its dignity and became no more than a heap of painted silk.

Alain's first words were for the two men. "Is this your land?"

"We works on it."

"Well, I must leave my air-ship here, the envelope and the car. See that no harm comes to it. Tomorrow I will send a wagon, to have it transported to my home."

The men expressed their willingness to guard the balloon, with broad smiles and much touching of the forelock. Now that they were convinced this was no supernatural threat or judgment on them they were cock-a-hoop with their own importance. Which of their fellows had ever sustained such an experience?

The stableboy rode off and caught Alain's horse, and Alain nodded in approval. "Good sense, lad, to bring a spare horse."

Marie's eyes filled with tears. She wanted to say, "I thought to bring the horse. I, not he," but knew this would sound mean and petty.

Alain left it to the boy to help Marie to mount, and the three of them set out on the journey back to Rippiers. To refresh the horses and themselves they stopped at an inn for a meal, and here, the stableboy naturally eating in a different room, Marie felt more free to talk.

She began by expressing her deepest concern. "Please promise me you will never do such a thing again!"

Alain looked puzzled. "Such a thing as what?"

She shuddered. "Going up in a balloon."

He laughed. "My dear girl, I intend to ascend frequently."

"Oh, no! It is so dangerous."

"Nothing of the kind, for an experienced aeronaut. I have been ballooning in France for several years. It's true there have been accidents, but many of them were caused by the hot-air balloons catching fire. Mine is inflated by hydrogen gas."

"It is still dangerous," Marie insisted, stubbornly.

"Why should my safety be of such consequence to you? I seem to remember your declaring that you hated me."

"I didn't mean it," Marie mumbled.

"Mean it or not, you had so little faith in me that you refused to tell me what your mother's letter contained."

This reminded her of the news she had to give him. "Alain, Peter is dead."

She expected amazement, even disbelief, but Alain's expression did not change, and she felt compelled to ask, "Did you know?"

"No."

"But you don't seem surprised."

"Why should I be? Such a woman courts disaster."

"She was shot."

"Then she must have been doing something unlawful."

"Alain, it happened on your land. Do you not wish to discover who did it? Should you not report it?"

"Where is the body?"

"Jenkin Sparks buried it."

"Ah, then no doubt he is the murderer."

"No! No, I am sure he is not. Alain, you must not get him into trouble."

"Why not? Isn't it my duty to bring a criminal to justice?" He looked so stern as he said this that Marie feared for Jenkin.

"You wouldn't want an innocent man to be convicted," she said, persuasively, "and I am sure Jenkin is innocent. Why should he tell me, if he had done it? He could have remained silent, and no one would have known."

"Well—" Alain hesitated, then went on, "Now you can retrieve your mother's letter."

Here Marie was in a quandary. If she told Alain that Jenkin had the letter, Alain would get it from him, would threaten him with exposure, might even pin the murder on him, and this Marie could not bear to have on her conscience. In the matter of the letter and the treasure he showed a ruthlessness she could not condone.

"Peter may have hidden the letter," she suggested, "or even destroyed it. I don't suppose we shall ever find it now." She almost wished this were true, wished the letter were buried with the depraved and unfortunate woman, as somewhere the treasure itself must be buried.

TWELVE

A few days later Alain's sister arrived. Marie had been slightly nervous, expecting an imposing personage, a haughty young lady ready to find fault with a girl raised in the alleys of Wapping. But Blanche was small and dark and plump, and did not put on any airs. Her accent was somewhat more pronounced than Alain's, as she had not come to school in England, but she spoke English fluently enough and was polite and friendly. Marie believed they could be good companions, and she felt happier than ever before in her life. The threat of Peter had been removed. Now she could roam the park and the woods in safety. As for Rippiers, it had completely lost its sinister atmosphere. Servants seemed to be everywhere, going about their duties, and Marie and Blanche filled the rooms with their chatter and laughter.

Soon the two girls had reached the stage of "Tell me about yourself," and Marie was pleased to recount the story of her life in full, and enjoyed the satisfaction of Blanche's expressions of wonder and exclamations of horror.

Blanche's life had been less spectacular. When her parents returned to France she had been little more than a baby, and her uncle's death coming so soon afterwards had robbed her of any memories of him. She had lived quietly with her parents. Alain had been educated in England, and once or twice the three of them had visited him. Then her father died, and later her mother. Now she had only Alain.

Marie was reluctant to speak of Blanche's mother, remembering how unfeelingly Gustave and his wife had acted towards her own mother, yet she was anxious to learn all she could about the family. "You knew of my existence?"

"Your existence?"

Marie smiled, to show Blanche that she bore her no ill-will on this account. "Your mother told you, before she died, that my mother was with child."

Blanche's round, baby-face seemed meant for laughter, yet now when she tightened her lips they were thin and straight. "Oh, I took little notice of that. When people are on the point of death they say many strange things."

"You felt no desire to find me?"

"A servant's brat? One would expect her to rid herself of it, either before or after birth."

"Blanche, that's cruel!"

"Life is cruel."

"But Alain came."

"Yes, he came."

"As soon as he knew where I was he came, and he saved me from Peter."

Blanche looked sharply at her. "You have a fondness for my brother?"

Marie was embarrassed. Her cheeks felt hot and she could not raise her eyes to meet Blanche's. "Of course! He is my cousin, as you are. You and I should be fond of one another, shouldn't we?"

"Yes, and I believe we are. But we must not brood on old family histories. There is only one thing the past can do for us. It can lead us to the family treasure."

"I don't care about it," Marie declared, gaily. "I know Alain is concerned, for my sake, but it's not of any great consequence to me. I am young. I can work. I won't be a burden on you and Alain."

"Vaudelets do not work," Blanche said, severely.

Marie looked surprised. "I thought everyone in France worked now."

"Our family does not recognise the Revolution."

"But these are modern times. There is no disgrace in working."

Blanche smiled. "You are so innocent. As for the treasure, that is not to be dismissed so lightly. Money is important. Please, Marie, trust Alain! Tell him what is in your mother's letter."

"I have forgotten."

She ignored this. "He will do what is best. You need his help."

"Truly I have forgotten."

"You are not being honest, Marie. Alain believes you remember, and he believes you have the letter, or you know where it is. Is that not so? Look at me, Marie! Look into my eyes!"

Marie looked, and was compelled to look away. How could she swear, when Blanche was partly right? She had forgotten that vital phrase in the letter, but she did know who held the letter.

"We are your friends," Blanche said, gently. "It is not good that you should deceive us." And she went softly away, her head drooping, as though sad and offended.

Marie found herself in a dilemma. To hurt and antagonise Blanche was the last thing she wished to do, and to hurt Alain was even more painful. Why was she withholding the one thing they asked from her, the thing they could all share? It was, she supposed, because she wanted no more conflict, no more danger of spring-guns, no bullet-ridden bodies. Jenkin had already been wounded by a trap intended for her. How could she expose him to further danger by confessing that he possessed the letter?

She thought about this as she lay awake deep into the night, and came to the conclusion that she must persuade Jenkin to hand over the letter to her, for in this way there would be no risk to him. It seemed simple there in the darkness, even simple when she awoke early and rose and dressed and went out.

Autumn was becoming well advanced. Marie had put a

warm shawl over her shoulders, and she drew it close about her as a chilly wind shot its needles into her.

She went towards the clearing, thinking Jenkin might still be in his cottage as it was so early in the morning, but before she reached it she heard the thuds of an axe upon wood and found him in process of cutting down some small trees.

She greeted him formally with, "Good-day to you!" and with scarcely a pause went on to ask, "What are you doing?"

He stopped and turned slowly to look at her. "Should be easily seen, even by a cockney."

"Have you been given instructions?"

"Instructions? Who would instruct me?"

"Monsieur Vaudelet."

He spat, but had the grace to turn his head from her as he did so. "I don't take orders from him."

"It is Vaudelet land," Marie reminded him, reasonably. "You can hardly go cutting down woods on your own responsibility."

He laughed. "I'd need to be a real Samson to do that. No, I'm just culling some of these self-sown saplings, the rubbish that's keeping the light and air from the good timber."

Marie shook her head. "I don't understand you. You say you don't like to work for the Vaudelets, yet you are tending the land, improving it."

"I don't rightly understand myself," he confessed.

"I shall tell Monsieur Vaudelet you are acting as woodsman and gamekeeper, and he must pay you properly." She spoke firmly, to show him that she was not prepared to stand any nonsense about pride, for, looking closely at him, she thought he had a thinner, more undernourished appearance. "Do you come down to the house regularly for your food?"

"No, I never come now."

"But that's ridiculous! What do you eat?"

"Rabbits. Birds. Hedgehogs, like the gipsies. Blackberries, hips and haws. I steal carrots and turnips from the fields. Autumn is a good living time."

"That's not enough to keep up your strength. You must come to the house each day."

"And be turned away by the la-di-dah servants?"

"The Mumbys will look after you."

He stared at her. "The Mumbys? Where are the Mumbys?"

"In their usual place, obviously."

"Have you seen them?"

"Well, no. But there are so many servants now. I rarely go to the kitchens."

"I can tell you, the Mumbys have disappeared, vanished completely, as if they had never existed."

"That's impossible."

"I've been to the house more than once. The cook shoo-ed me from the kitchen. Then a footman threatened to kick my—kick me out."

"They wouldn't leave. They have nowhere to go. Mr Mumby told me so. I expect they have retired to a room at the top of the house, an attic where they can be alone and at peace."

"Anyway, I've not set eyes on them."

"I will make inquiries, and I will give orders that you are to be provided with a meal each day and with food to take away."

"Do you think your orders will be obeyed?"

"Of course! Jenkin, you have the wrong idea of the Vaudelets. You have become embittered because your own life has been hard. Alain is just and honourable, and you would find no one sweeter and kinder than his sister Blanche. We are great friends."

"You are fortunate," he said, but there was something in his voice which made her feel that he spoke ironically.

"I shall tell Monsieur Vaudelet that you are working hard and must be paid a fair wage."

"Why should you bother with me?"

It was difficult to answer. He was a stubborn young man, prickly and uncivil. He did not take kindly to being helped,

and gratitude seemed foreign to him. She supposed she pitied
his poverty and loneliness, having known both herself. "If I
make these arrangements for you, will you do something for
me?"

"Ah!" Reciprocal benefits he recognised. They were a part
of the survival of the underprivileged.

"Will you give me my mother's letter?"

He replied to this with another question. "Did you know
Monsieur Vaudelet has been here?"

"Yes. I rode through the woods with him."

"Since then. Two days ago. He also wanted the letter."

"You didn't give it to him?" She was surprised at her own
alarm. Why shouldn't Alain have the letter? Didn't she
herself want it in order to pass it on to him?

"No, I didn't give it to him. He tried to bribe me, and then
to threaten me, but I didn't give it to him."

"I don't believe you!" she cried, angrily. "Alain wouldn't
stoop to anything mean, like bribery and threats. I don't
believe—"

"That he would visit me, ask for the letter, without telling
you? You have great faith in some people."

"But not in you," she flashed. "You are making this up,
from spite. You want to discredit Alain in my eyes."

"Yes, for your safety."

"That is nonsense. I am in no danger, now Peter is dead.
Give me the letter!"

"I will not."

"Well, tell me just the two words I have forgotten, the
words my father said to my mother when he was dying."

"Those two?" Jenkin laughed, but his expression was one
of anger, not amusement. "Those are the only words that
matter. D'you think I care about the rest of the scribble?
D'you think I care about your mother's wantoning with a
fine gentleman? Only two words in that letter have any
meaning, and you'll not hear them from me."

"You heartless beast!" She was so furious that she wanted
to hit him, but he still had the axe in his hand, and she had

the feeling he might not hesitate to use it on her. "You're just a good-for-nothing vagabond. I shall tell Monsieur Vaudelet to send you away, dismiss you from Rippiers."

"And lose the letter for ever?" he mocked.

"Oh, damn the letter!"

She was shocked at herself, shocked that she could have said such a thing, so shocked that she turned and ran, without uttering another word. Why did the horrible young man have such a bad effect on her? Certainly she would not mention Jenkin Sparks to Alain, would not petition for food or wages for him.

On one point, however, she did wish to be informed. "Alain, what has happened to Mr and Mrs Mumby?"

"Oh, they have left. Didn't you know?"

"You promised you would not turn them out."

"Nor did I. I assure you, my dear cousin, they went entirely of their own free will."

"But where? They had nowhere to go."

"A relative offered them a home."

"Mr Mumby said he had no living relations."

"That was what he thought, but I understand that a nephew turned up. I forget the details, but I think it was from Canada, where he has done very well. He will be able to give them every comfort."

"They didn't say goodbye to me."

"Perhaps they thought you would be otherwise engaged. They are shy people."

"I would like to have seen them before they left."

Alain took her hand in his. "You are so tender-hearted. I admire it in you, Marie, but sometimes I fear for you. You are very vulnerable. You need someone to protect you."

Her heart swelled with affection and gratitude. Here was her sanctuary, with Blanche and Alain. She must take no notice of people like Jenkin, poor troubled souls shaken by malice and jealousy. She shared the blood of the Vaudelets, and in them she could trust.

THIRTEEN

As the last autumn leaves parted reluctantly from the trees
and the birds puffed themselves up against the cold, Marie
wondered what it would be like, her first winter at Rippiers.
She had heard that the gentry did a considerable amount of
entertaining, and half expected a gay round of balls and
concerts. When no invitations were sent or received she was
surprised. It seemed a waste, having a large staff of servants
to wait upon only three people. Yet she did not like to ask the
reason for this, for fear Blanche and Alain might think she
found their company inadequate.

In truth she was happy and contented. There were the
blazing log fires to which they returned after taking their
exercise of walking or riding, the bright illumination of scores
of wax candles, the rich leisurely meals. Blanche played on
the pianoforte and had a pleasing voice. Alain had a stock of
puzzles and conundrums, and both brother and sister were
fond of cards.

There was, however, one matter which Marie found
inexplicable, and that was Blanche's habit of going out of the
room, often for an hour at a time. She would get up from the
fire for no apparent reason, put her hand on Marie's
shoulder and say, "Well, I will leave you two for a while.
You and Alain must have a lot to talk about."

Marie was bewildered. Surely she and Blanche had more
in common, more to talk about. They could talk of fashion
and needlework and cosmetics and flowers and herbs and all
the many female occupations which seemed trifling to men,

whereas with Alain it was difficult to find a subject on which they could meet.

Marie would plead, "Oh, no! Stay, Blanche!"

But Blanche was adamant, and her absence would leave an emptiness in which silence itself became an oppressive weight. Alain slouched in his chair, and sometimes Marie suspected he dozed.

Yet for all this the time passed pleasantly enough, and at Christmas they made an effort to be especially gay, and at night entertained the servants to a feast worthy of royalty. Marie looked to see Jenkin among the party, but he was not there. She felt a pang of regret at the thought of him in that dark and dreary hut, but it passed almost immediately. No doubt he had been invited and refused. Why should she waste pity on a man so cross-grained and unbending?

In January the weather worsened, and most of the time they were confined to the house. Blanche's songs and piano pieces lost their charm through familiarity, Alain's puzzles had been solved again and again, and Blanche and Alain exchanged sharp words over the card games. Marie ascribed their irritability to close proximity, and was careful not to provoke them.

One day as she came down the staircase she heard loud voices and saw the sister and brother in the hall, apparently in the course of a quarrel.

Blanche was saying, "You will have to do it, I tell you, you must!" Her voice was strident and her face distorted.

Alain, as though searching for a reply, glanced up and discovered Marie. "Ah, cousin! You look nervous. Do not take any notice of us." He moved forward and took her hand as she reached the foot of the staircase. "You are frozen. Come to the fire. There is a north-east wind and it is beginning to snow."

Blanche passed them without a word and went upstairs, and Alain led Marie into the dining-room, escorted her to a chair and walked to the window and gazed out.

Marie felt that an apology was due, though she had done nothing wrong. "I'm sorry I disturbed you and Blanche."

He shrugged his shoulders and spoke without turning. "I am glad you did. We were in the midst of one of our arguments. Lately, it seems, we can agree about nothing."

"In the summer you were good friends."

"Yes. In France we were never together as much as we are now."

"I hope it's not my fault."

"Yours?" He swung round and approached the fireplace. "How could it be yours? You are even-tempered and good-natured, as a woman should be. Blanche is more excitable and petulant, but she is practical as well. Though she is younger than I, I would do well to take her advice."

"What has she advised now?"

"Oh, nothing of importance."

He cleared his throat and started to speak, but broke off and continued to watch the flames.

After a few minutes Marie asked, "What were you going to say?"

"Nothing. Nothing at all."

He looked so troubled that Marie pitied him. "What were you going to say?" she repeated.

"Well, there was something. I think we should talk about your future."

Her heart missed a beat. So that was it! That was what Blanche meant when she said, "You will have to do it." He was going to tell her she must leave Rippiers.

"What about my future?" Her voice shook a little.

"You are drifting, are you not? Nothing is decided. You have no plans and no definite place in the household."

"I have told you, I want to find work."

He dismissed this with a gesture. "I took you from filthy and sordid surroundings, and was thankful to be able to do so. But by my action I transferred you to an alien environment. My responsibility lies heavily on me."

"Why should it? You have made me happy and safe."

"Is that enough? Do you not feel your life is aimless?"

Suddenly she was angry. "Of course I have no intention of staying here for ever, dependent upon you, upon your charity. As soon as the worst of the winter is over I shall go and look for a situation. Or if you prefer it," she added, "I will go before the end of winter. I will go tomorrow. I will go today."

He stared at her in alarm. "Oh, no, Marie! That is the last thing I would want. Did you imagine I meant you to leave here? Do not suggest such a thing! Do not even dream of it!"

"What did you mean, then?"

He sighed. "I was coming to that, but the words have jumped out of my mind and bounced away."

She waited quietly, but inwardly she was impatient.

"What I want," Alain swallowed, then spoke so quickly that Marie could barely understand him. "I want to ask you to marry me."

She said the first thing that came into her mind. "Why?"

"Why what?"

"Why do you want to marry me?"

"That's no answer," Alain told her, irritably. "I asked you a question. You've no reason to question me in return."

"I have. I have reason."

"Which is?"

"A proposal of marriage should be—should be—"

"Oh, yes! It should be preceded by a passionate declaration. I should swear that I cannot live without you. I should write a sonnet to your hair, and certainly your hair is worthy of a sonnet. But the French are a practical people, as well as being logical and intelligent. Were my parents alive they would in all probability arrange a suitable match for me, but since they are dead I must do it for myself."

Marie roused herself. "I'm no match for you. I'm badly brought up, and only half educated. You wouldn't be proud to introduce me to your friends."

"I would be proud to take you anywhere." With a slightly

awkward movement he went down on his knees in front of her. "Must I make pretty speeches in order to convince you?"

"No, I don't like speeches. But you haven't told me you love me."

"Would I ask you to marry me if I did not?"

"You might. You are French. You believe in these marriages of convenience."

"Love is a spoilt word," Alain declared, scornfully.

"It's the only word we know for offering our heart and all of ourselves to someone for ever. It's the only word, whatever language we speak."

"Oh, you English are stupid romantics!"

Her eyes filled with tears. "Alain, are you proposing or quarrelling?"

"Marie, you must be sensible."

"I don't want to be sensible."

"At least give me your answer."

"I can't, not yet. I must think about it. Please leave me alone!"

He left her alone for the rest of the day, and most of the time Blanche also stayed out of sight. Try as she might, Marie found it impossible to think clearly on the subject of Alain's proposal. Her brain felt as woolly as the snow that continued to fall, and her feelings towards Alain were those of resentment and embarrassment and disappointment.

She retired early, but as she climbed into bed and prepared to extinguish the candles, there came a knock at the door.

It was Blanche. "May I speak to you?"

Marie's first impulse was to send her away, to pretend to be sleepy, though she knew well she would lie awake, perhaps for hours. This was her problem, not Blanche's. Blanche would be prejudiced.

That was when curiosity caused Marie to hesitate. Of course Blanche would be prejudiced, but in which direction?

She patted the bed. "Please come and sit down."

Blanche made no attempt to mince matters. "Alain is extremely unhappy."

"Unhappy?"

"Of course! What do you expect of a lover who hangs in suspense?"

"Blanche, he is practical. He told me so. He believes in the French method of arranging marriages."

"Play-acting."

"What?"

"He is a proud man, and shy of showing his feelings. If you refuse him, it will break his heart."

"I cannot believe that."

"He loves you passionately."

"Wait a minute, Blanche! Surely you are exaggerating."

Blanche took Marie's hand. She looked very sweet sitting there in the light of the two candles, very sympathetic. "Dear cousin, you know so little of men. But I have been out in the big world. I have seen them. They cannot bear to show their feelings as women do. They fear that they will become dependent, hostages to fortune, will lose their manliness if they disclose their need for love. Marie, I know my brother far better than you do. He is a real man, jealous of his strength and authority, but deep within him he is crying to possess you, to cherish you."

When Blanche fell silent Marie did not know what to say, and Blanche had to urge her, "Tell me, Marie! Do you not care for Alain?"

"Oh, yes, I do! I am extremely fond of him."

"Then tell him so. He is longing to hear it. And if you must consider the practical side—"

"Blanche, I'm not concerned with the practical side."

"All the same, let us consider it. What better destiny for the Vaudelets than that they should unite? We are the last of them, you and Alain and I. You are my cousin, and I would welcome nothing more greatly than that you should become my sister-in-law."

To this gracious persuasion Marie could find no reply. It was an honour that both Blanche and Alain should desire a close relationship with her, she who was a nobody compared with them. How could she be so churlish, so ungrateful as to refuse?

One last doubt she voiced. "Blanche, have you ever been in love?"

Blanche laughed. "A score of times."

"Then tell me, in what way do you recognise love? How do I know that I love Alain?"

"Can you contemplate hurting him, ruining his life?"

"Oh, no, I would not want to do that."

"Then you love him."

She stood up and brushed Marie's forehead with a light kiss. "Good-night, dear cousin!"

Marie and Alain were married in the church at Rye, when the spring equinocial gales were blowing. From the sea the wind crossed salt-marshes and sand to attack the little town on the rocky hill. It roared like thunder round the walls of the old building, and in the crevices it whistled with an almost human voice. Marie found herself listening to it, and for her it drowned the words of the marriage service.

FOURTEEN

As Marie had told Blanche, she was fond of Alain and wanted to be fair to him, so she had to confess to herself that he had in no way deceived her. He had spoken of marriage as of an expedient and a congenial state, and she would be foolish to expect from him more than he was prepared to give. He was business-like, both in and out of bed, and treated her much as he had done before the wedding. There had been no question of a honeymoon, and he showed no desire to be alone with his wife. Blanche spent the whole of each day with them, making no excuse to leave them by themselves.

The coming of spring was a joy to Marie, she having seen few signs of it in the stones of the city, but in Alain it seemed to engender a peculiar restlessness. She was troubled by this, and thought it might be due to the strain of a marriage so devoid of expressions of affection. Perhaps he mistrusted her feeling for him. Perhaps it was for her to reach out towards him, release those emotions which would truly unite them.

She attempted in the warm darkness of their bed to rouse his passion to something above mere masculine satisfaction, caressing him, professing a hunger which, even while she did it, she knew was no more than simulation. It embarrassed both of them, turned him from her in disgust, with, "Have you no womanly reserve? You are behaving like a whore."

It was enough. Burning with shame, she resolved she would lie still as a statue whenever he made what was falsely called 'love' to her.

Several times, during the first month or two of marriage,

he had questioned her about her mother's letter, until, weary of giving him the same reply which he did not believe, she sat at her desk and wrote down every word she could remember.

He read it, and burst out, "What is the use of this rubbish?"

"What do you mean, rubbish?"

"Why, all this about a secret wedding and being turned out by my parents when my uncle died. Is it not obvious what happened? Your mother left of her own free will when her lover died and there would be no more favours from him. As for the child—as for you, you were begotten on the mud of some alley, or against a tree in a boulevard."

"That is a lie!"

"How can you say so? You can prove nothing."

"I have written down my mother's letter."

"But not the part about the treasure."

"That I have forgotten."

"Convenient!" he sneered. "Very convenient. But it will do you little good now. You are my wife, and what is yours is mine, so you may as well tell me."

"I would, if I could remember."

"Why should you forget that one thing?"

"I don't know. Perhaps it's because it had nothing to do with the rest of the letter. It was just two odd words. Alain, what must I do to convince you? By what shall I swear so that you know it's the truth?"

"I would not believe you if you swore by every saint in the calendar."

"I am not familiar with many of the saints. Oh, Alain, why won't you forget it? You have all the money you require, and I need no more, now that I am married to you."

He laughed. "Let me tell you something. I have none, no money at all. I am ripe for bankruptcy."

"You are joking."

"Have you known me to make a joke about money? Money is no jesting matter."

"But—but it can't be true. The family fortune—"

"Vanished with the Revolution. When my father took us back to France, he found his lands had been distributed among the peasants the Vaudelets had once employed. It was impossible to retrieve them. The chateau, crumbling and decayed, was of no value without the land. Only one true friend remained to him, the banker with whom he had deposited capital, stock and bonds. There was sufficient for us to live quietly, as any middle-class family. But my father was not a quiet man. He was used to keeping up a certain style. He sent me to school in England, my sister to a ladies' school in Paris. He had to have servants, to see my mother dressed according to her position. There was not sufficient money for all this, and so he gambled. When he died there was nothing left. My mother had nothing to live on, nothing to live for. Her death came shortly afterwards."

Marie was bewildered. "But you made money."

"I? What means have I for making money? You know I detest work."

"Then how do we live here? The servants, the horses and carriages, the beautiful things you have bought. The very food we eat, the—"

"Save me the list! It's a long list, as well I know. I will tell you how we do it, my little simpleton. We do it on credit."

"Credit?"

"Indeed, yes! Rippiers is a large house. In England I can still call myself the Marquis de Vaudelet, and the English are impressed by titles. Would they expect me to have my pockets weighed down with coppers, or to walk around carrying a bag of sovereigns? No, I order everything I want, and the more I order, the less incumbent is it upon me to pay. Valuable paintings, tapestries, who but a wealthy gentleman would buy such things? Balloons, who but a gentleman of substance would indulge in such a whim?"

"They must be paid for sometime," Marie pointed out.

"Ah, there you have found the plague-spot. There comes a day of reckoning, and that day is close upon me. The tradesmen are becoming impatient to have their accounts settled, the servants are growing restive to be paid their wages."

"But you knew this would happen," Marie said. "Why did you do it?"

"I had no alternative. And why should I be troubled about the future? Anything may happen. The world may end. The treasure may be found."

"That is why you are so concerned about the treasure."

"It is. And, believe me, it is no mere legend. Great-grandfather was not only a shrewd man, but he was something of a miser as well. He suspected his son, my grandfather, to have spendthrift tendencies, and so he did not tell him where the treasure was hidden. Instead, he gave the secret to his eldest grandson, Uncle Rodolphe."

"My father."

"The man you say is your father. He never told my father, though they were brothers, and it caused bad blood between them. When I was a small boy I used to hear them quarrelling. Now you understand, Marie, why it is essential I should find the treasure."

"Oh, yes, indeed! I will do everything I can to remember. When a thing is known to us it is never really lost, is it? It can come back, even after years."

"It had better not be years, in this case," Alain told her, grimly.

"But if it should—if by mischance I should never remember, it won't be so bad. You could sell Rippiers to pay your debts."

"What a little fool you are!" he exclaimed. "Pay my debts with the price I should get for Rippiers? It would be like trying to irrigate the desert with a teaspoon of water."

The thought of such debts filled Marie with a sense of helplessness. She looked down at her fashionable gown. Was this hers, or was it in fact the property of Miss Grey?

"I will send them back," she said, impulsively.

"Send what back?"

"The clothes Miss Grey made for me."

"What good would that do?" Alain asked, wearily. "Do you imagine she could find a use for second-hand dresses and mantles and bonnets? Bankrupt I may be, but even though I go to prison we must cover our nakedness."

"Oh, no! No, Alain! That could not happen. They could not really send you to prison, could they?"

"Many better men than I, many nobler born, have ended their lives in a debtors' jail."

"That you shall not do," Marie declared. "I shall obtain the letter for you. I promise. We shall find the treasure and everything will be all right."

"You are a good girl."

"I am your wife." For the first time for weeks she was glad and proud to say this. It was as if Alain had come back to her. Now she believed she understood the reason for his recent moodiness and lack of attention. He had been racked with anxiety, desperate at the situation in which he found himself. She remembered her first sight of him, in her prison-room at the Leather Bottle. To her he had been a creature from another world, smelling of perfume and pomade.

This memory brought in its train another one. "That bag of sovereigns you gave Peter to set me free, you could ill afford it. I wonder where it is, now that Peter is dead."

Alain laughed. "Do not fret yourself about that. It was play money, stage money."

"What do you mean?"

"Counterfeit. Oh, do not look so puzzled, Marie! Did you really think I would buy you with a bag of gold?"

"Am I not worth it?"

"No woman is worth a bag of gold. But I expected to have bought with you the secret of the treasure."

"And so you have."

"You have remembered the two words?"

"No, but I shall get the letter from Jenkin."

Alain's face dropped. "That," he said, sourly, "is empty confidence. I should have insisted that the woman handed over the letter before I gave her the money, but I was in a hurry."

"Because you had cheated her."

"I had every right to cheat a villainess."

To Marie this sounded doubtful morality, but she was at that moment more concerned with the events following her escape. "Then it was you Peter was following, not me. But why did she chase me through the woods and later over the fields?"

Alain shrugged his shoulders. "Perhaps she had the intention of holding you as hostage. She would believe that without the letter and without you it would be impossible for me to find the treasure. Perhaps she had hopes of seeking it for herself."

"Alain, did you—" She stopped. She had been about to ask, "Alain, did you marry me because of the letter, because of the treasure?" But that would have been an unforgiveable question. Whether his answer were "yes" or "no" it would mean the end of her marriage, in so far as trust and affection entered into it.

Quietly she left him, and went to her room to put on her bonnet—"Miss Grey's bonnet," she said to herself—and then made her way through the gardens to the outer park and the woods.

So much had come to light during her conversation with Alain that her head was spinning. A few words had reduced him from a wealthy man to a pauper and a debtor, but this had not lowered him in her eyes. She had felt compassion and a longing to help him. But then had come contempt that he should cheat Peter, even though Peter had been worthy of nothing else. Most wounding of all had been the suspicion she dared not voice, that her marriage had literally been one of convenience for Alain, that he was using her for the purpose of retrieving his fortune.

Not only was her pride hurt, but it was as if a chilling frost had penetrated the depths of her nature. She was eager and ready to give love and warmth, she who had known so little of love in her life. Alain had appeared as her saviour. Had he offered greater encouragement she would have bestowed on him her whole heart. Now his image wavered and broke, as though someone had thrown a careless stone into a pool of clear water. What to think she did not know, but what she must do was simple. Alain was her husband, and her duty was to help him.

She reached the edge of the clearing, and saw a thin coil of smoke rising lazily from the chimney of the hut.

The new grass, fresh and green where Jenkin had cut and cleared it, swished soft and cool about her ankles. She crossed to the hut and knocked on the door.

There was no sound from within and she knocked again, disappointment beginning to creep over her.

The door opened with such a flurry that it was as if Jenkin had been standing right behind it. He pulled it shut, and asked, "What do you want?"

His tone was far from welcoming, and Marie's voice faltered as she replied, "To speak to you."

"Well?"

He seemed poised ready to go, and she had the urge to put out her hand and hold him. Instead, she suggested, "If I might come inside—"

"No. I am busy."

She tried to joke. "I don't mind if it is untidy. Men are often bad housekeepers."

"You can say what you want to say here. Better still," he gave her a little push, "let's talk under the trees."

"Why are you so anxious to get me away from the cottage?"

"You shouldn't be here at all."

"Why not?"

"I suppose he sent you, your husband."

"No, but there is no reason why he should not. Why are you so hostile? He allows you to live here in peace. He—"

She was angry, and she raised her voice, and then broke off as someone spoke from inside the hut, feebly but clearly.

"I know who that is," he said. "Let her come in."

FIFTEEN

Mr Mumby was lying on a low bed in a corner of the room. Marie had to cross over and bend down before she could recognise him. Spare and frail he had always been, but now he was so emaciated that his bones stood out whitely, as though about to pierce the flesh.

"Mr Mumby!" Marie exclaimed. "What are you doing here?" It sounded a foolish question as she asked it, for the answer, she thought, grimly, would be, "Dying."

Jenkin replied for the old man. "I brought him. He managed to get back, and I found him wandering in the woods. I had to carry him. He weighed next to nothing."

"Why did you leave your nephew?" Marie inquired of Mr Mumby. "You and Mrs Mumby were comfortable with him, weren't you?"

The old man stared at her, but Jenkin laughed. "What nephew?"

"The one from Canada. The one who has done well for himself."

"Oh! That one!" Jenkin exclaimed, ironically. "I'm sure that one made them very comfortable, seeing as how he don't exist."

"What do you mean?"

"I can guess who told you that cock-and-bull story. When the monsieur turned 'em out they had to go to the workhouse, and that's where Mrs Mumby died."

"Oh, no!"

"Oh, yes!" Jenkin contradicted. "What did you expect from your fine lord, your fine husband?"

"He promised—"

"Promised? When did he ever keep a promise? When did any Vaudelet ever keep one? They're rotten, all of them."

"That's not true. Have you forgotten I'm a Vaudelet?"

"No, I've not forgotten."

The old man was making signs to them, waving his arms in the air. "Listen! Can't you listen to me?"

Marie leaned towards him. "What do you want to say?"

"I'm so tired. There's not much time, and it's for both of you, something you must know. I can say it, now she's gone. I can—" he stopped, fighting for breath, and Marie lifted him up.

"Can you raise the pillow?" she asked Jenkin. "Now, Mr Mumby, take it slowly. Don't exert yourself. We are listening. We won't quarrel and swear at one another."

"No need for that," Mr Mumby murmured.

"What did you say?"

"No need. You're both Vaudelets."

Jenkin started forward. "What's that? What's that bosh? You're rambling. That's what it is. He's rambling."

"Hush!" Marie commanded.

"She was a good-looking woman when she was young, was my wife," Mr Mumby went on. "He happened to see her one day, and she took his fancy."

"Who happened to see her?" Marie asked, gently.

"The old marquis. Not the oldest marquis, you understand. He was still alive, but was getting on in years. The old marquis was young then, and Rodolphe and Gustave were little boys. Fine little chaps, aged four and five or something like that. Well, the old marquis got Mrs Mumby with child, only she wasn't Mrs Mumby then, and so he felt responsible."

"As responsible as he'd feel for his swine. Less than he'd feel for his horse."

"Be quiet, Jenkin! Go on, Mr Mumby."

"He wanted her to be settled in life, and he picked on me. I was an undergardener at the time, and he told me he'd look after me if I'd marry her. I said I'd be honoured."

"Honoured!" Jenkin cried. "I'd have spat in his eye. Anyway, what's all this got to do with us?"

"The child was your father."

"My father!" Jenkin sat on the bed so suddenly that it shook and rocked. "My father!" he repeated. "My God! A Vaudelet! That's the worst news I've had."

"It's not so bad," Marie said, encouragingly. "You'll get used to it, like I did."

"I never shall."

"So Mrs Mumby was your grandmother. Now I see why she was so anxious to look after you and nurse you."

Mr Mumby waved his hand again to attract their attention. "Women is funny. I weren't ashamed, but she was, and she never let it be known that the child was hers. The old marquis was proud of the boy, in his way, and made him gamekeeper."

"My father hated the Vaudelets," Jenkin said, fiercely.

Mr Mumby shook his head. "Not always. Not until they went back to France. He was angry then, because they didn't take him with them, and it was him, Jenkin, as put you against the family."

"I don't need any putting against 'em."

"That's foolish, hating your own blood," Mr Mumby said. "Mrs Mumby turned against the child, her being proud and feeling the marquis had wronged her. It was put out to nurse and brought up by one of the lodgekeepers. But you, Jenkin, after your father died she began to feel for you."

The old man looked so exhausted that Marie urged him, "Rest, Mr Mumby! Please rest!"

He shook his head, and a faint smile touched his lips. "I got plenty of time for rest. I got all the time in the world." He glanced at Marie, expecting her to smile in turn at his small, pathetic joke, and she did so, though she could have wept to see a man so spent that he clung to the shreds of life only because he must say what must be said.

"I will come back," she promised.

"That'll be too late. There ain't much more to say, only that Mrs Mumby done wrong and she were bitterly sorry."

It was difficult to picture Mrs Mumby as a young girl lovely enough to take the fancy of a French nobleman, but years fell heavily on fair and foul alike. "I expect she loved him very much," Marie said, excusing her. "It wouldn't seem wrong to her."

At what appeared to Mr Mumby to be rank stupidity a spurt of strength returned to him. "I weren't talking of that. That weren't wrong. A woman can't say no when a fine gentleman casts his eye on her. I was saying about Mrs Mumby doing wrong when she laid that trap with the wire and the gun."

"Mrs Mumby did that?"

"She saw you going to the stables, and reckoned it would get you on the way back"

"She did it? Not Peter?"

"She couldn't know as Jenkin would come that way. I could have told her, 'cos I met him earlier, but she never told me of her plan, never told me till she was dying, in the workhouse."

"But why me?" Marie asked, confused. "What harm had I ever done her? Why would she want to kill me?"

"Mrs Mumby thought the Vaudelets was all dead, and so did I. The lawyer, he stopped sending us our wages. We seemed to be forgotten, and Mrs Mumby she said this was Jenkin's chance. He's the last of the Vaudelets, she said. She wouldn't let me tell you she was your grandmother, Jenkin. She just said if we was to keep quiet, one day the house and estate would be yours. Then Monsieur Alain arrived."

"Did she hate him?" Marie asked.

"In a way. She was afeard of him, anyway."

"But how could I be a threat to her?"

"Well, she knew Monsieur Alain would marry you."

"That's ridiculous!" Marie exploded. "How could she? We were scarcely acquainted. I had only met Monsieur Alain a couple of times."

"She knew," Mr Mumby insisted. "Maybe she had the second-sight, or maybe it was what anybody would expect, a young man and a young woman living in the same house." Mr Mumby gave a small, weary sigh. "It preyed on her mind, and her mind was getting muddled."

"Well, thank heaven she did not kill anybody. Now you must try to sleep."

Jenkin followed her out of the hut and across the clearing. "He won't last long."

"I know."

"Now you can understand that Peter was not as bad as you thought."

"She was bad enough." Marie turned to face him. "What about you? You've discovered you too are a Vaudelet. What about that?"

"It's a bit of a shock," he admitted.

She hesitated, then said, "Jenkin, I need that letter more than ever now."

"So does Monsieur Alain. Oh, yes, he told me many things when he came to see me. He told me he was ruined, and he promised me half the treasure if I would give him the letter."

"Oh, no! Surely he didn't do that! He wouldn't, because he knows the treasure is rightfully mine."

"Do you think that would stop him? When he found he couldn't bribe me, he threatened to kill me, but that was stupid, because he'd never get the letter then. I laughed in his face. Then he told me something else. He said he married you to get the treasure, not for any other reason."

She opened her mouth to say, "That is a wicked lie!" But the words never came out. An icy cold ran through her. She shivered, and her legs trembled so that she had to put out her hand to hold on to Jenkin. At that moment she knew Jenkin was speaking the truth, and knew, moreover, that she had always known it. From the first sight of Alain the seed of knowledge had been sown deep down inside her, but a seed is small and takes time to grow.

She closed her eyes, as if to blot out something almost too

painful to be borne, but it was there, in her heart and in her head. She had to accept it. She opened her eyes and looked at Jenkin. "Men marry for a number of reasons," she said, bravely. "Alain was honest with me. He told me that in his family and his country marriages were arranged. But that wouldn't prevent people, afterwards, growing to love each other."

"Do you love him?"

"He is my husband. I have a duty towards him, especially now he is poor."

"That wasn't what I asked. And he isn't poor. He's in debt, which is a different matter."

"Even so, I must help him. He needs me. His sister too. Blanche is not to blame for his foolishness."

"They are both young and healthy. Isn't it possible they could work?"

"I don't think it is," Marie replied. "They haven't been brought up as we were. I think they were led to believe they are superior beings."

"Then it's time they learned they are common clay," Jenkin said, roughly.

"They can't, not all at once. Jenkin, please give me my mother's letter! If you will, you shall have my share of the treasure. I promise this faithfully, and you can trust me."

"I believe I can." There was surprise in Jenkin's voice, as if he had just made a discovery. "And what will you do?"

"Well, I am not really interested in riches." She spoke almost apologetically. "Anyway, Alain offered you half of the treasure, so he must have intended to share his portion with me."

"Why should he?"

"I am his wife."

"Oh, what a simpleton you are!"

"Jenkin, there are wicked and cruel people in the world, but you're not one of them. You know that letter belongs to me. You know I should have it."

"You can't, as it happens. After I buried Peter I burned

the letter. I thought it best to put an end to all this nonsense. You say you're not keen on wealth and possessions. So it won't trouble you, will it, to leave the treasure lying wherever it lies?"

"No, it won't trouble me. But Alain—"

"I'll tell you something else, then. When he hears from you that the letter has been destroyed, he will have no more need for me, will not hesitate to kill me."

":Don't be ridiculous! Why should Alain kill you?"

"He doesn't like me very much."

"If we killed everyone we don't like very much," Marie said, vigorously, "there would be far fewer people in the world. Alain wouldn't kill anyone. He is far too sensitive and civilised."

"What about Peter?"

"You've no reason to suppose Alain did it."

"He or one of those he employs. What does it matter? Listen, Marie, I have put my life in your hands. Will you tell your husband about the letter?"

"I don't know. I haven't thought."

"Then here is something else to think about. Before I burnt the letter I memorised—no, not the letter, but just two words."

Suddenly Marie was terribly afraid. She clapped her hands over her ears. "Don't tell me! Don't say them!"

"I must." He took her by the wrists and pulled her hands away. "You're not the only one who has a duty." He gazed at her sternly. "I have a duty towards you. The words are 'Forty Footsteps'."

PART THREE

Field of the Forty Foosteps

ONE

Slowly Marie walked back to Rippiers. Questions darted through her mind, and found no answer. The two words kept time with her in a heavy beat. "Forty footsteps. Forty footsteps." They made a poor marching song, she thought, one which weighed down the feet instead of lifting up the heart. Why should two words have such a sad and sinister sound?

She threw herself down on the grassy slope of the hillside. She must try to think clearly, not become confused. First, should she tell Alain of the forty footsteps? Of course she must! That above all was the practical and sensible thing to do. Alain desperately needed money, otherwise he would find himself disgraced, perhaps even imprisoned, and Alain was her husband. It was as simple as that. What, after all, had Alain done? Threatened Jenkin? That had been mere talk, mere bluff. Killed Peter, or had Peter killed? There was no evidence. Jenkin could as easily have killed Peter, during a quarrel or to get sole charge of the letter. Alain was blameless, except— Marie tried to put the thought of the Mumbys out of her mind. Probably Alain had believed they were provided for, had no knowledge of their destitution, of the workhouse?

She sprang to her feet and ran lightly down the hill, anxious to find Alain and tell him the good news, but there was no sign of him.

In the small upstairs study she came upon Blanche, who was standing by the window. "Where is Alain?" she asked.

Blanche did not turn, and Marie went over to her. "What's the matter?"

Blanche tried to keep her face averted, but it was obvious she had been crying.

"What has happened?" Marie insisted. "Tell me!"

"Where have you been?" Blanche asked, in a choked voice. "You've been gone a long time."

"I couldn't help it. There was something I had to do."

"The servants have all walked out."

"Good heavens! Why?"

"Isn't it obvious? You could not expect them to work for ever without wages, with no hope of wages."

"Well, where is Alain?"

Blanche spun round, unmindful of her reddened eyes. "He is in his balloon, crossing the Channel to France."

For a moment Marie saw only the humour of this. "I hope he doesn't expect me to follow with the horses, to bring him back."

"It is your fault," Blanche declared, angrily. "If he is killed, you will be responsible."

"I? How? I never wanted him to go up in that foolish airship."

"It is worse that that. It is more dangerous. He has made a bet with a man he knows, a wealthy Frenchman, that he will cross the Channel and descend by parachute."

"By parachute? Is it possible?"

"Oh, yes! It is possible. I think Monsieur Garnerin was the first, or one of the first, to descend successfully—oh, about fifty or sixty years ago. Since then a number have tried. Some have been hurt, some have been killed."

"Why is it so dangerous?"

"I do not understand all the scientific reasons, but the wind is the greatest peril. When it blows hard the basket is tossed violently from side to side, the aeronaut has no control over it. He may be dashed against rocks or trees, or it may strike the ground too violently."

"I wish I had come back sooner," Marie said. "I would have prevented him from going."

"You!" Blanche exclaimed. "You could not have moved him from his purpose. Everything you have done has been bad for him. I wish he had never found you."

"You approved of our marriage."

Blanche drew herself up. Her eyelids were swollen and her nose was red, but she achieved an effect of great dignity. "I suggested it."

"You mean—"

"I mean that Alain sent for me in despair. When he told me everything I saw at once that he must marry you, so that he might secure the treasure for himself when you led him to it."

Humiliation swept through Marie. "He did not desire me for his wife?"

Blanche smiled. "He was not—how do you say it in England?—over head and ears in love."

"I thought he had a fondness for me."

"You failed him."

"I felt—I had affection for him."

"But you kept your secret."

"I forgot the words. Now the letter has been burnt."

"Then we have no hope."

Suddenly Marie was angry. "Money!" she exclaimed. "That is all you think of, you Vaudelets. Nothing is of value to you unless money will buy it. Well, I'm not greedy for dead men's treasure. I will share it with you, or you may take the lot if you are too avaricious to resist it. The clue to the treasure lies in two words. Forty footsteps."

Blanche threw out her arms and gripped Marie by the shoulders. "What do they mean, those words?" Her eyes were shining.

"I have not the least idea."

"You must have!"

"They were spoken by my father as he lay dying. My

mother wrote them in her letter which was brought with me. Who knows their meaning?"

"It must be possible to decipher them. Think!" Blanche urged, impatiently. "Consider their meaning. What are footsteps? They are paces, and forty must be a measurement. But from what point to what place?"

Marie sighed. "One might speculate for ever."

Blanche walked up and down the room. "The information was intended for you. You must solve the puzzle."

"But I know nothing of the family, except what you and Alain have told me. We can only surmise that Great-grandfather hid the treasure somewhere around here, in the house or the grounds. If we could find some name, some reference—" She clapped her hands. "I know! The library! Perhaps in an old book we shall find the clue."

"Good gracious! It will take ages," Blanche complained.

"The more reason to get started," Marie said, energetically.

She was glad enough to shut herself away. It would be several days before they knew whether Alain had safely concluded his reckless mission, and to have something with which to occupy her mind would help to pass the time.

For two days she persevered. Her eyes grew tired, for often the print was faded or the pages browned, according to the age of the books, and her young limbs ached from the unnatural effort of sitting motionless hour after hour. She began to wonder how long she must continue before abandoning her search. Certainly she could not examine every book in the library. It was quite possible that the information she needed was not there. Perhaps because of the incompleteness of the message the treasure would lie undiscovered for ever.

By a strange but by no means uncommon quirk of fate, Marie was within an ace of giving up the search when she found the clue she needed. It was in an account of the Duke of Monmouth's rebellion that a legendary story of two brothers was mentioned. Being on opposite sides they quarrelled, and fell to fighting so ferociously that they killed each other, and afterwards, in the field where they fought, the mark of their feet persisted, and over these forty footsteps no grass or other vegetation would ever grow. Even when the field was ploughed, it was said, the footsteps could not be obliterated.

Marie went to Blanche in triumph. "I have found it!" she cried, and related what she had read. "The Field of the Forty Footsteps. That is what my father meant. That's the key to the treasure."

"Well, where is this field?" Blanche asked.

"In London."

"London!"

"Yes, behind Montague House. At least, it was there. But nearly seventy years ago, in eighteen hundred, the fields were built over. They are now all streets and houses."

"What is the use of that?" Blanche demanded. "Do you suggest we go to London and buy up all the houses and demolish them, in the hope that the treasure may lie somewhere in their foundations?"

"No, but it must be a clue."

"If it is, it is a mockery."

"I'm sure there is something in it," Marie persisted. "Forty footsteps is so definite a number, not a phrase which could apply to various things. So forty footsteps must refer to Monmouth's rebellion and the two brothers. The story is not far short of two hundred years old."

"You are a fool!" Blanche exclaimed. "If Great-grand-father hid the treasure before they returned to France just over twenty years ago, the streets and the squares and the houses were already built. Where, then, was the field of the forty footsteps?"

"But he wouldn't wait until then to bury gold and jewels," Marie said, excitedly. "Alain said he had among them some gems from the crown jewels of France. Don't you see, he'd want to get them safely out of sight when he first arrived in England, during the French Revolution. He'd be afraid of being followed, of having them stolen from him, and at that time the fields were still open, no buildings on them. Here's a quotation from the diary of Joseph Moser." She picked up the book she had brought from the library and began to read. " 'June 16, 1800. Went into the fields at the back of Montague House, and there saw, for the last time, the forty footsteps; the building materials are there ready to cover them from the sight of man.' Great-grandfather could have hidden the treasure before that happened."

"And sat back, here at Rippiers, knowing that tons of stone were rising over his fortune, so that he would never be able to dig it up?" Blanche sneered. "I do not think he would have been so foolish."

Marie's high spirits evaporated. "What would he have done?"

"Rescued it. Placed it somewhere else. Who knows?"

"It would be worth investigating," Marie insisted. "We should go to London."

"How? Walk all the way? We have no coachman, no servants to carry our baggage. Worse, we have no money."

"Oh! I had forgotten."

"So we wait here until Alain returns, and then we shall at least have a stable-boy."

"A stable-boy?"

"Of course! Alain trained him to manage the balloon, so that it could be brought down safely after Alain went over the side with his parachute. Did you imagine he would abandon the balloon, allow it to be wrecked? Such conveyances cost a great deal of money."

"I had not thought of that," Marie confessed.

"No. You may have knowledge of Latin and Greek, but in many ways you are exceedingly simple."

Marie could not believe that her careful research had been wasted. "Alain will go to London when he returns," she said, confidently.

"If he returns."

"Had there been an accident, we should have heard."

"Perhaps."

Both girls were silent. They had little in common, and there was not now a great deal of sympathy between them, but at that moment the same thought had crossed their minds. Could not a balloon be a way to freedom? Would it not offer a happy escape to a man whose debtors would shortly be snapping like hellhounds at his heels? Did Alain really intend to return?

TWO

The two girls took it in turn to watch the sky. They did not discuss their fears and anxieties, and Marie did not know when Blanche's hopes began to run low. She only knew that with each passing day the chance of Alain's return seemed to become more remote, and when two weeks had gone she felt it was time to abandon a foolish and pointless vigil. Yet she hesitated to suggest this to Blanche, for fear of inflicting pain on her.

From Blanche's white and drawn face it was obvious she was suffering great distress. Hard and mercenary she might be, but her devotion to her brother was genuine.

For herself, Marie realised, circumstances were different. The growing suspicion that Alain had married her in order to secure the treasure had been confirmed by Blanche's confession to having contrived the marriage, and this had given the finishing stroke to her relationship with Alain. She understood now that she had never loved him. But, love or not love, Alain was her husband; nothing could change that.

During those two weeks of waiting, she saw nothing of Jenkin, and was slightly bothered that he had not come to see how they fared. She almost decided to go and seek him out, but was reluctant to do so. It was pride that stopped her, she supposed. Jenkin was a rude, unco-operative man, and she had an idea that for some unknown reason he disliked her.

The third week of Alain's absence dragged by, and Marie could stand it no longer. She went out to the drive in front of the house. Blanche looked very small, very lonely, as she stood there, head tilted skywards.

"It's no use," Marie said. "He won't come."

Blanche swung round, tense, furious. "How dare you say that! It is not true."

"We must face facts," Marie insisted. "It is time we made inquiries, discovered what has happened."

"Oh, it is all very well for you. You do not wish Alain to return. You hope he has been killed, so that you may claim the treasure for yourself."

As she spoke, there came the sound of carriage wheels and horses hooves. She broke off, and both girls were silent. So quiet and secluded had their lives been in the past weeks that there was something alarming in this simple occurrence of an arriving visitor.

They had to wait until the vehicle had passed the dense border of shrubs, and then they saw the carriage was a fine one, newly painted, drawn by a pair of white horses, with a coachman in a colourful uniform, and two liveried footmen behind. But these things they scarcely noticed consciously, for seated in the carriage was Alain.

It drew up. The footmen jumped down. One opened the door while the other unfolded the steps, and Alain alighted. He said to the footmen, "The stables," waving his hand carelessly in that direction, and walked towards the two girls. He was dressed in the latest Parisien style, and he looked like a prince.

Blanche threw herself into his arms, sobbing with joy. "Alain! Oh, my brother! Thank God you are safe!"

"Did you think I would be otherwise?" he asked, lightly. "I made a considerable stir in France, I can tell you! There they have a proper respect for aeronauts. I was a hero to them."

"I do not want you to be a hero. I want you to be alive."

"And alive I am."

She pulled at his arm. "Come inside! You must be tired. You must be hungry."

"You do not want me to recount my exploits?"

"Later."

"Marie will not want to hear. She does not admire balloons or those who fly them. Do you, Marie?"

"I think they are dangerous."

When he saw the food they put before him he gave it a look of disgust. "What is this? It is a meal for servants."

Blanche apologised, but Marie was angry at his lack of perception and consideration. "What do you expect?" she asked. "We have no servants, so we are servants. Also we have no money with which to buy fresh provisions."

"No money?"

"Are you surprised, considering you left us none?"

He laughed. "That can soon be remedied," he replied, taking a handful of gold from his pocket and flinging it across the table.

"So you won your bet."

I did indeed. I hurled myself from the balloon in my parachute, floated like a wisp of thistle-down and alighted as gently as a bird. Fortunately there was little or no wind. The boy descended a mere two miles away."

"Where is he now?"

"Oh, he has bettered himself. He has taken a position in France. The ladies were scratching out each other's eyes in a battle to engage him. They say he is so fair and handsome that his descent from the skies must be a supernatural event. My balloon and parachute are being despatched and should arrive in a few days."

Blanche gazed at him. "I wish you were not so brave."

"But you wish me to provide money."

"Of course!"

"Now we will engage more servants, and replenish our food supplies, and order some fashionable clothes for the three of us. I declare, you girls look as dowdy as country mice."

"Will there be money for all that?" Marie asked.

"Indeed there will."

"After you have paid your debts?"

"Who mentioned the payment of debts? What a little

bourgeois you are, Marie! But since you mention it, the procedure is this. I pay my debts, or a portion of them, and order more goods. In that way the tradesmen are satisfied and I am relieved from worry, and so everyone is happy."

"But you will not have money with which to pay for the new things."

"Who cares about that?"

"It is not honest."

"She is teasing you," Blanche said, sharply. "She knows there will be money, because she is on the way to finding the treasure."

Alain sat up straighter. "Now that is good news. You see, I am starting a run of good luck. Tell me about it, Marie Annette! Tell your loving husband exactly what you have discovered."

It was so long since he had called her Marie Annette that she was carried back to the days when she first knew him, when he had seemed splendid and without blemish, and a wave of sadness washed over her.

"What would you say if I refused to tell you?"

She spoke idly, yet from a melancholy curiosity arising out of her disillusionment. But she was not prepared for the expression of rage which contorted his face. He looked like an animal about to attack, and instinctively she drew back, away from him.

"If you refused, I would—" He stopped abruptly and regained control of himself. "— I would feel disappointment. I would persuade you to reconsider. Even in England it is for a wife to obey her husband."

"I was joking," Marie assured him, hastily. "I had no intention—" She went immediately to fetch the book, and showed it to him, and repeated the two vital words, being careful to mention the fact that she had been given them by Jenkin.

Alain's face darkened again. "I knew that bastard was holding back the letter."

"No. The letter has been destroyed. But the words are correct. I remembered as soon as I was told them."

Alain brooded over the brief account. "Duke of Monmouth. Two unnamed brothers. Montague House. What have these things to do with us?"

"I don't know. But don't you think you should go to London to find out?"

She held her breath as she waited for his reply to her suggestion, and was surprised at her own anxiety. Why should she wish to be rid of Alain? Why should she urge him to go away as soon as he arrived home? This was no way for a wife to treat her husband. Had he become so insufferable to her? Or was her overriding emotion one of fear? She felt guilty that such ideas should have occurred to her. "Perhaps not, though. Perhaps you can learn nothing in London."

"What can I learn here?" he asked, pettishly, and demanded of Blanche, "Why did you say she had the clue to the treasure?"

"I said merely that she was on her way to finding it."

"It is all poppycock and moonshine. My uncle must have been delirious. Dying men say foolish things. Forty footsteps, indeed! Perhaps he said nothing of the kind. Perhaps he spoke in French."

"Then we can give up the search. We need not trouble ourselves." The cheerfulness in Marie's voice was not assumed, for a part of her was conscious of relief. Failure to find the treaure might prove a blessing. She and Blanche and Alain would turn their hands to honest work. They would sell Rippiers to pay some of the debts, and the three of them would go out with hope and courage to earn their living. If Alain stayed with her, remained faithful to her under those conditions, she would know that something of value had developed between them, even though he might have married her for mercenary reasons.

But perversely Alain chose to oppose her. "I might as well go and see whether I can pick up any information. Someone may have heard the story, may add something to it, offer another clue. Besides, I have business to do in London, purchases to make. I shall engage my new staff while I am there. I have no love for the local people."

He went off in the grand carriage, with the coachman and the footmen, despite Blanche's request that one of the men should be left behind to help in the house, and Rippiers settled back into quietness.

Blanche was in a strange mood, as anxious as any of them for Alain to find an answer to their riddle, yet only too ready to blame Marie for sending him away.

"Anyone would think you have a lover," she said, spitefully. "You seem much more at ease when you have rid yourself of Alain."

"If I have a lover," Marie told her, "then I see little of him, for I am with you almost every moment of the day."

"There is always the night."

"And when do I sleep? I would be yawning all day."

Blanche merely shrugged her shoulders. She was such poor company that Marie felt compelled to seek the solace of the books in the library.

For a private and neglected library it was a fairly large one. Now as she looked up at the laden shelves she could not help wondering whether there might somewhere be another reference to the field of the forty foot-steps. Surely such an odd legend merited further notice. But where to find it?

Patiently she searched the books dealing with the districts of London, particularly during the previous two centuries, and eventually in an account of London theatres found that at the Tottenham Street Theatre, some forty years back, a melodrama had been produced bearing the title, "The Field of Forty Footsteps."

She was excited by her discovery, but could not see where it would lead her, until in a footnote she found, in very small print, that a book by Jane Porter, published in 1828, was called, "Coming Out, or the Forty Footsteps."

By now she had spent nearly four whole days in the library, and she really could not see how these extra scraps of information could help. If history led only to a dead end, what use would melodrama and fiction be?

Yet she wheeled the heavy library steps across the room and climbed to the top of them. An obscure melodrama was unlikely to have survived in print, but early nineteenth-century novels were not so plentiful as to be discarded lightly.

She found the book, and scrambled down the steps, proposing to read every word. As she did so, a piece of yellowed paper fell out of it. Almost she ignored this, until it occurred to her that it might serve as a bookmark. She stooped and picked it up. The writing on it was faint but legible. It was only three lines. "Rye," it was written, "N.E." On the next line was, "King Field," and on the third, "Dead Man's Lane."

She seated herself in one of the big leather chairs and began to read the book. It was not until she had passed twenty pages that a thought struck her. How could she expect to find a clue here? Miss Porter would have known nothing of Great-grandfather and his secret treasure. It was true that Great-grandfather had known something of Jane Porter, for he had possessed her book, but when the novel was published, in 1828, the field concerned had been built upon for nearly thirty years. Certainly Great-grandfather could not then have read of the legend and gone to the field which no longer existed.

It was so confusing. It was— She sat up straight. Of course it was not confusing! It was obvious. Forty Footsteps had not referred to the field, but to the book which had been written about the field. In that book he had concealed his secret.

She took the paper in her hand, carefully this time, for it was precious. Dead Man's Lane and King Field, to the north-east of Rye. After all, Great-grandfather's treasure was where one would expect it to be, near to home.

THREE

Exuberant as an excited child Marie flew to Blanche with the news of her discovery, book and paper clutched to her as though she would never let them go.

"This must be the clue our great-grandfather left. See the writing, how old and faded it is. And the title and the subject of the book follow the words my father said to my mother."

Blanche was surprisingly calm. "We will show it to Alain when he returns."

Marie stared at her. "Wait until he comes home? He may not be back for another week or more. I simply could not endure such delay."

"It is our duty to do nothing until Alain instructs us."

When Blanche spoke with such decision and formality it was difficult for Marie to remember that Alain was her husband and that hers was the right to decide what to do in his absence.

"I suggest we search for the treasure."

"Walk out into the country with spades in our hands?" Blanche asked, contemptuously. "How do we find this place, this Dead Man's Lane?"

"We can inquire. Surely the local people will know."

"Oh, yes! Have the whole population of Rye standing around and watching us as we dig. Have I not told you before that you are a fool?"

"Yes, many times, and sometimes you are right. Of course we cannot let everyone know of our discovery. I had not thought of that."

Blanche turned to face her. She looked concerned, almost distressed. "You have a better nature than I have, Marie.

You do not take offence. I say unkind things to you, and still you are friendly."

"Are you trying to make me vain?"

"No, I am telling you to—to be careful. You do not deserve that any harm should come to you."

"Harm?" Marie was amazed. "What harm could come to me now? Peter is dead, and so is poor old Mrs Mumby."

Blanche did not seem anxious to enlarge on the reason for her warning, and as Marie reflected on the best course to take, an idea occurred to her. "I know! Jenkin! He can tell us where the place is. He can help us search."

"Jenkin Sparks? Oh, no!"

"Why not?"

"You must not trust him."

"Jenkin is entitled to part of the Vaudelet fortune, and I am willing to share my portion with him."

She did not stay for further argument, but went out and up through the woods to Jenkin's hut, still armed with the book and the paper.

Jenkin listened and read and nodded. Marie watched his face as he did so. There were no signs of excitement, nor was there the disquiet she had seen in Blanche. His expression was closed, secretive. As he did not say anything she was compelled at last to prompt him. "Well?"

"Have you told your husband?"

"I can't. He's away, in London, looking for information in the place where the field of the forty footsteps once was."

"Ah! And his sister?"

"She knows."

"What did she say?"

Marie hesitated, then admitted. "She warned me against you."

"In what way? What crime am I expected to commit?"

"She didn't mention anything specifically."

"I suppose my most likely action would be to grab the treasure and make off with it."

"If I had thought that," Marie pointed out, "I wouldn't

have asked you to help me. Anyway, some of it will be yours."

"I don't know that I want it. There may be blood on that gold."

"Why? No one has been killed on account of it."

"Not yet. But some things are best left buried."

"Now you are being fanciful," Marie said, practically. "Will you help me?"

"I suppose I must. Someone needs to." He spoke grumpily, but he fetched a spade and pickaxe and they set off.

"What is the meaning of the names of the field and the lane?" Marie asked.

"Oh, there's an old story that once when the Danes invaded this part of the coast the inhabitants fought with them in a field, and afterwards the bodies of those that were killed were buried in a lane close by."

"Dead Man's Lane."

"That's what they say. Who knows what truth there is in old tales?"

It had sounded simple, reading the instructions on the paper, and they had no difficulty in finding the lane, but when they reached it they stood, at a loss, wondering where to begin.

"To dig up the whole lane, 'twould take us a month of Sundays," Jenkin complained.

"Perhaps there are some mounds," Marie suggested.

"How many did they bury? If a hundred were slain, would you mark a grave for each one?"

"At least," she said, consolingly, "they haven't ploughed up this lane."

"But hedges have grown, and trees."

"Perhaps they buried the dead on the side nearest the field."

"Perhaps. Perhaps not. Anyway, we are looking for treasure, not corpses."

"I thought Great-grandfather might have put it where the men were buried, else why did he chose this place?"

"It's easier to ask questions than answer them."

"Well, the treasure wasn't buried so very long ago, not like the men after the battle. If we try somewhere where there are no trees, and the grass is not so thick—"

They decided on a likely-looking place, and then another, and then another. Jenkin broke up the ground, and Marie removed the loose earth. They worked until they were tired and hungry, but all they achieved was a number of hillocks of fresh soil which looked as though a family of moles had been busy.

"We'll come again tomorrow, "Marie said, at last.

Jenkin laughed. "How many tomorrows?"

Back at Rippiers, Marie reported to Blanche their lack of success. "I have an idea there's a clue we have missed," she added, "something we've not taken into account."

She went to the library, as though hoping that the very presence of books would inspire her, but they had nothing to offer. The information had been given, was there on the paper placed in Jane Porter's book, undisturbed for so long. Yet an essential detail had been omitted, either carelessly or cunningly. To designate an area as considerable as a field and a lane, and to give no intimation as to the exact spot, was merely to tantalise. Perhaps, after all, the lane had been mentioned as a pointer to the field, instead of the opposite. She was not an expert judge of sizes, but she supposed the field to be all of five acres. Added to this, it had been tilled through the centuries. If the treasure lay there, it lay deeply.

She expected to lie awake pondering her problem, but the hard physical work had tired her, and she fell into a sound sleep almost immediately, to waken only when a bar of morning sunshine fell across her bed.

She felt refreshed and alert, as though no puzzle could be too difficult to solve. The answer must be there, on the paper and in the book.

She sprang out of bed. Something was coming into her mind. It was almost as if she heard a voice, her father's voice, speaking two words. Forty footsteps. Yes, but how could one

pace a field that was practically a rectangle? The possible
directions were legion. But, wait! Her father had spoken of
footsteps, not of a field. To step out forty paces from either
end of a narrow lane would be a simple procedure, and the
area to be examined would be only as wide as the lane was
wide.

She was too excited to eat any breakfast. "Today we shall
find it, Blanche. I know we shall."

"You must take some food, otherwise you will not have the
strength to dig."

"There won't be much digging to be done." She was
completely confident. "Blanche, come with me! You should
be there when we unearth the secret. It will be a wonderful
moment."

"No, I'll stay here, in case Alain comes. Marie, I wish you
would wait for him. He has a right to be present."

Inwardly Marie acknowledged the truth of what Blanche
said, but she feared the consequences of Alain and Jenkin
coming face to face over a pile of gold and jewels. Better to
give Jenkin his share, and then take the remainder to Alain.
They had had no indication that Alain might return that day,
but Marie was conscious of a sense of urgency. They would
find the treasure, she was convinced, and she was also
convinced of the need of haste.

When she reached the lane Jenkin had not arrived, and to
save time she measured the forty paces, taking the longer
strides she would attribute to a man. Barely had she done this
before Jenkin came, this time carrying two spades. He looked
happy, she thought, and she was not surprised. Who would
not be happy expecting to lift riches from the earth? But even
as she ascribed this reason for Jenkin's cheerfulness, she
knew it would not be valid for her, and doubted if it would be
for him. For him and for her great wealth would be excessive.
Alain would know what to do with it, but they would not.

Jenkin held up the spades. "See! We can both move earth
today, for there will be much earth to move."

"No." She shook her head, and told him of her new

theory. "This is the place I've calculated. If we take about six feet on either side I'm sure we shall find something."

For a time they worked in silence, the mounds of soil growing beside them, and as nothing came to light Marie's conviction wavered. "Perhaps after all I'm wrong."

"At least we can carry on, up the bank."

"There's a tree in the way."

"An ash. Only a small one, a sapling." He caught hold of it, and his hand could almost encircle the trunk. "This hasn't been growing for more than fifteen years. Maybe a bird dropped the seed, or the wind blew it."

Carefully he removed the earth from around the base, then dug into the roots. "I don't want to kill the tree if I can help it."

Marie stood watching him. There was no room for both of them to work, and she found it pleasant to look at the easy rhythm of his movements. He was stronger than she had imagined, for in spite of his slim build he seemed to labour without effort.

When his spade struck something solid, Marie gave a little cry.

"Maybe just a stone," he warned her, and scraped away the loosened earth. "Now would you believe it," he said, softly, and whistled.

Marie leaned forward. The roots of the tree were exposed, and between them, pierced by them, intertwined with them, lay a human skull. Again she cried out, but this time with a mingling of amazement and horror and awe. "Look! The tree has grown right through it. Is it very old?"

"I don't know. Perhaps a thousand years."

"We shouldn't have uncovered it."

He sat back on his heels, looking down. "It isn't always good to uncover things. Marie, d'you want to uncover this hidden treasure?"

"Of course! Don't you?"

"What will you do with it?"

"Give some to you, and the rest to Alain, to pay—" She

broke off, realising it would be disloyal to disclose the fact that Alain was in debt.

"What will you do afterwards?"

"I haven't thought."

"Live like a Vaudelet, I suppose, with your husband and his sister, ride horses others groom and saddle, eat food others cook, enjoy everything second-hand. It doesn't sound much of a life to me."

"What will you do with the money?"

"I'd like to refuse it," he admitted, "but I'm a poor man and I can't afford to make grand gestures. So I'll take it, and I shall buy a farm and be my own master."

"That sounds good," she said, wistfully.

"You could do the same."

"Somehow I can't see Alain as a farmer."

"Nor can I. I'd like to know, for sure, whether you really want to find the treasure."

"Yes, I do."

"Then here it is. I've caught a glimpse of it." Cautiously he raked away more of the soil, and the whole of a skeleton was revealed. Beneath its left arm, wrapped in rotted sacking, was a box about a foot long and some eight inches wide.

"He shouldn't have done it!" Marie cried. "It was mockery, to put it there. Dead men don't need gold and jewels."

"But it does them less harm than it does some living men. Crimes! This is heavy. It's lead, I reckon."

He was sweating when he had lifted it out and placed it in front of Marie.

Marie hesitated. It was an ugly, dirty box. Difficult to believe it contained the beauty of gold and diamonds and the blue and green and red fire of other gems.

"Well?" Jenkin demanded. "Aren't you going to open it?"

"She would be wiser if she did not," said a voice. "I will take charge of it."

Startled, they looked up and saw Alain standing a few feet away.

Marie went to him. "Isn't it marvellous! We have found it."

"Marvellous indeed! You may go now, Sparks. You have done your job. Marie Annette, run to the house, and come back with the carriage and horses. Bring a footman, too. I doubt if the old coachman can lift that box alone."

"Jenkin will help him."

"I do not require Sparks further. Now do as you are told."

"No, Alain!" She clasped her hands tightly together, as if to give herself courage. "Jenkin must have his share."

"Share? Who spoke of shares?"

"Then he can have mine."

"Little fool! As your husband I own every one of your possessions."

Slowly Jenkin got to his feet. The spade was still in his hand. "I'm not going to see you rob her. You've done her a bad turn as it is, marrying her. I know your sort. You'll take everything from her and then throw her out. My father held there were no good Vaudelets. I say there may be some, but you're not one of them, and I'm not going to let you lay a finger on whatever is in that box."

"And how will you prevent me?"

Jenkin went towards him. He was holding the spade as if it were a weapon. Marie was not sure what he intended to do, and instinctively cried, "No, Jenkin!"

Her warning was unnecessary, for Jenkin never reached Alain. Alain took out a pistol and fired it, and Jenkin fell to the ground.

FOUR

The box lay open, its contents winking in the sun, their value something to take away the breath of an assessor, but to Marie they were no more than the glass beads on a market stall in Wapping.

As she started forward to go to Jenkin, Alain's hand came out and fastened on her shoulder, digging into the flesh. With the toe of his boot he had lifted off the lid of the box, and he stood motionless, staring down, the pistol still in his right hand.

"You have killed him!" she cried.

"I expect so," he agreed, carelessly. "But if he is not quite dead, he soon will be."

She struggled. "Let me go!"

"Quiet, girl!" He shook her. "Stay where you are or I will shoot you as well. I really have no preference, one way or the other, except that it might be a little embarrassing to explain the disappearance of my wife. As for him," he nodded towards Jenkin, "he will not be missed. He is of no consequence. If he is not dead, then he will soon bleed to death. I do not think people use this lane frequently." He took his hand from her shoulder, but warned her, "Stay perfectly still. I meant what I said about shooting you."

"I must see whether he—" Marie choked on the words, and stopped. Her eyes filled with tears, and the jewels at her feet seemed to break into a thousand reflected lights.

Alain knelt down and began to stuff the coins and gems into his pockets. "This box is too heavy to move, but I think we can manage the stuff. Here, take this!" He threw into her hands a collar of emeralds and a tiara exquisitely set with diamonds as icily pure as frozen lilies. "It is fortunate I have pockets fitted for use and not merely for show, though I doubt if they will take all. What shall I do? Ah, yes! The rest can be carried inside my shirt." Soon the box was empty save for one coin. Alain took it out and balanced it on his finger, a golden guinea. "Shall I leave this as a peace-offering to the gods? Would you like it, my poor penniless fellow?" He addressed the skeleton. "Would it make your bed any softer? Ah, well, my need is greater than yours, so I'll keep the money." He stood up. "I feel as heavy as an ancient knight in armour. Lead on, Marie Annette! I do not think we should waste more time."

She turned to him, holding out the jewels. "Take these! You can have everything, but let me stay with Jenkin."

"With a dead man?"

"He is not dead. I have just seen him move."

"And you have a fancy for him?"

The question was like a blow. She came to life, trembled with life and understanding. "Yes," she said, "I have a fancy for him."

"What a pity you will be disappointed! You are my wife. Had you forgotten that? You are my wife and you are coming with me. Now go! Move!"

He drove her as if she had been an animal. Once when she stumbled he hit her on the side of the head with the butt of his pistol, hard enough to make her cry out with pain, but not hard enough to render her unconscious.

She tried, as they went, to make some kind of plan for escaping from Alain. Surely when they reached Rippiers it would be possible. She would appeal to Blanche to reason with Alain, and if that had no effect she would beg her to go to Dead Man's Lane and do what she could to save Jenkin. But Rippiers was not Alain's destination. He made a détour across the park, skirting the house and the stables, to a field at the back, and as they approached she saw, above the hedge, a great golden globe that moved and trembled slightly in the breeze.

Her first sensation was one of lightness and relief. Alain was going away. He was preparing to escape from her, from Rippiers, from his debts, and now from the consequences of his crime in shooting Jenkin. Well, let him go!

She thrust the collar and the tiara into his hands. "Have these as well," she said, "I don't want them."

She would have left him at that spot, but he pushed her through the gate into the field. The balloon was anchored, and beside the car stood a small group of men, waiting. Among them she recognised the footmen.

Alain managed to thrust the two pieces of jewellery into his shirt with the others, caught her by the hand and dragged her across the field. With the weight he carried, his attempt to run was ludicrous, especially as Marie was pulling away from him.

"Take the ropes!" he called. "I am ready to leave."

The men did so, dispersing from the group, removing the grapnel-iron, holding tightly to the ropes as the balloon began to strain at them.

It was only then that Marie fully realised Alain's intention. "I am not coming with you."

He laughed and did not reply.

"I tell you I am not coming. Nothing will make me. You can't force me."

Had the men still been grouped around the car she might have appealed to them, but they were in a scattered circle, each holding a separate rope. She screamed, and one or two of them moved uneasily, but they knew that if they relinquished the ropes the balloon would be lost, and no man cared to take the responsibility of leaving his post.

"The lady is a little nervous," Alain shouted. He laughed as he told them this, and the men dutifully laughed with him. Most of them were married, and so they knew that women could be contrary and stubborn. If Monsieur Vaudelet wanted to take Madame Vaudelet for a cruise through the

clouds, and if Madame Vaudelet were somewhat reluctant—well, it was none of their business.

The top of the basketwork of the car was breast-high.
Alain lifted Marie and flung her in, then jumped after her.
She did not see him give the signal to let go, because she was
lying in the bottom of the car. There was no movement, and
for a few moments she thought that Alain had changed his
mind.

Not until she had picked herself up and looked over the
side did she realise what had happened. Below her was the
ground, with the men looking up, but it was a considerable
way below, and was dropping rapidly. She could not believe
the balloon was rising, for there was no movement, no
sensation at all. There was only the earth falling away, the
people becoming a few inches high and then shrinking to
specks, the ground becoming a chessboard, the houses like
pawns, Rye a child's fort, and the Channel a beautiful blue
wrinkled silk, the coast of France bounding it and transfor-
ming it into no more than a wide river.

In addition to the lack of perceived movement, there came
upon them a silence so absolute that Marie was afraid to
speak. Earth-sounds died away, and earth-sights became
misty and unreal as they reached the level of the clouds.
Clouds drifted past them, rolling, spreading, changing their
shapes to the forms and colours of a dream, while an
avalanche of snowy fragments pelted them, looking like white
rocks, but having no weight, no substance. Now, as Marie
looked down, the earth appeared only intermittently through
a tear in an apprently solid feather-bed of clouds.

"How high are we?" She whispered as she would have
done in church.

"Almost two and a half miles."

"Oh, please, Alain, may we descend?"

"Not yet."

"I'm sure we are high enough. We should go down before
it is too late."

He laughed. "Too late for what? Do you fear we may

mislay the earth, lose it, drift off to the moon? I tell you it is not as simple as that. In a balloon a man feels free, but this is a delusion. In reality it is still a captive balloon, held to earth by the chain of gravity. It will be a clever aeronaut who breaks that chain."

"I don't want to break it," Marie wailed. "I like to be on earth. I want to go down." As they were speaking they drifted from brightness into a dark cloud, grey and cold. "I can't feel any life in my hands. they are frozen. Why didn't you wait for me to fetch a warm wrap? Why did you not warn me we were taking to the air? You must have known. The balloon was prepared."

He nodded. "I knew. Last night I arrived—"

"Last night!"

"Yes. It was late. I left the carriage some distance from the house because I did not want to wake you. This morning, as soon as you had gone, I spoke to Blanche, and I knew I should be requiring the balloon, so I gave instructions that it should be inflated and made ready for flight."

"But not supplied with food and drink."

"There was no time for trivialities."

"I am desperately hungry."

"That is the fresh air." He drew a deep breath. "Oh, how clean it is! Uncontaminated by mankind, pure as the Garden of Eden."

"There are clouds," Marie said, practically, "and clouds are drawn up from the waters of the earth, so they could be fouled by earth substances. I've heard of a storm of frogs falling to the ground."

"Then perhaps we should go higher, where the air is too rarefied even for clouds."

"Oh, no!" Marie cried, in alarm. "We dare not go higher."

"Dare not?" he asked, scornfully. "A mere two miles? Balloonists have risen to four and a half miles and descended safely."

He sounded jubilant, almost, Marie thought, as though he were tipsy. Had the height affected him, or was he drunk with the sight and the touch of the jewels he carried? She even wondered if he were sane. Had a madness been growing on him, unnoticed by Blanche and herself?

As she pondered on these things she became more frightened. How could she persuade him to take them safely back to earth? She must be careful what she said, try not to anger him, because of the popular belief that madmen must be humoured.

"Are we going to France?" She tried to sound calm and matter-of-fact.

"We must already have gone three parts of the way."

"Then why not descend to a lower altitude, that we may see where we are?"

"No. We cannot."

"Surely it would be more sensible—"

She realised it was a mistake to argue with him, for his face flushed and he flew into a rage. "Hold your tongue, woman! I am captain of this vessel, and I say we must not fall below two miles."

"If you cannot see the ground—"

He grasped the edge of the car and leaned over, and the car tilted and rocked, causing the balloon to dip and leap sideways like a startled animal.

"Be careful!" Marie cried. "Oh, Alain, if you do that you may fall out, especially with the weight in your pockets and your shirt. Why not take out the money and the jewels and put them in the bottom of the car?"

"Oh, yes, you would like that!" he said, mockingly. "You would like to get your hands on them, would you not?"

"No, I would not. I would rather see a nice green field a few feet below me than all the jewels in the world."

His unstable mood changed again. He was in a good humour. He leaned forward and winked at her.

"It needs only for the clouds to break and I shall know whether I am over good French soil. The wind is getting up, so soon I think we shall have a clearer view."

He was right. The balloon seemed to come to life, and its

majestic, unobtrusive motion gave way to a movement which was swift and uneven and made Marie feel slightly sick. She sat clinging to the side of the car, closing her eyes to the dizzying antics of the clouds which were opening and streaming past.

She had no idea how long this nightmare race would continue, and it was a relief when Alain exclaimed, triumphantly, "There!"

She dared then to look down. Land was below, but oh, so far below!

"Let us descend at once," she said, urgently.

To her astonishment Alain did not open the valve as she expected. Instead he began to throw out ballast. This was provided by bags of sand each weighing six pounds. When the first one went, Marie was too dumbfounded for speech, but when the second and third went, and the balloon leapt upwards, she shouted, "Stop, Alain! Stop! What are you doing?"

He took no notice, but he heaved over the fourth bag. Marie caught at his arm, and he thrust her away with his elbow, throwing her against the side of the car. Slowly she picked herself up.

"That will do," he said. He was out of breath but he spoke pleasantly. "Now I can descend."

"*We* can descend," Marie corrected him, thnking he had forgotten she was there.

"No. I." He pointed to some ropes going down the outside of the car. Marie had not noticed them, but there were many things she did not understand about balloons. "My parachute is attached, beneath the car. That is the way I shall descend."

She was aghast. "You would not go and leave me here, alone in the balloon? Oh, Alain, you couldn't do it! You couldn't be so inhuman."

"I shot Jenkin Sparks. You still do not know me very well, do you, my little Marie Annette?"

"You cannot enter the parachute from here."

"Oh, yes, I can. I go down this special rope."

"I won't release you," Marie panted. "I won't pull the—what is it they call it?"

"The latch-cord. But there is no need for you to do anything. I am using the system devised by Mr Cocking. There is a rope running from the latch to the parachute car, which I myself will pull. And now there is nothing for us to do but say au revoir. Or should it be adieu?"

She flew at him, clung to him, in a hopeless, desperate effort to prevent him by force. For a moment he let her cling, and then he laughed. "If that is the way you prefer it, I can throw you out. It is only an act of mercy that I am allowing you a little more time to live. But perhaps—"

It was enough. She backed away, cringing, able to retreat so small a distance, pressing her back against the side of the car.

"If you impede me in any way—"

"I won't! I won't!" she promised.

"Strange, is it not, what people will do to live a few moments longer? The wind has changed. Isn't that fortunate? Fortunate for me, I mean. It is coming south-south-east, so you will drift back over the Channel."

She scarcely heard what he said, for she was watching what he did, watching his hands on the ropes. "You are opening the valve!" she cried.

"Yes, a little. Not too much. I want you to come down over the sea. That is the neatest, cleanest ending. I would not wish people to find a wrecked balloon and a mutilated girl. You are too beautiful, Marie Annette, to be broken and torn."

She thought, It will be all right. When he has gone I will close the valve. But he took a knife and cut the rope, too far up for any possibility that she might reach it.

"I think that has provided for everything," he said, with satisfaction, and calmly climbed over the side of the car.

She heard nothing, saw nothing, but when he pulled the latch and released the parachute, the balloon leapt upward like a shying horse, and Marie knew she was alone as she had never been before.

FIVE

The balloon began to drift back towards the English Channel, and as it went it lost height, steadily and imperceptibly. At first Marie did not look down. She clung to the side of the basket and prayed. The very fact of being alone in the balloon filled her with panic. She was convinced that at any moment the airship would explode or would suddenly and instantly deflate. It seemed impossible that she should still be alive, floating calmly over the earth, so near to people who could help her, yet so far from the feasibility of obtaining their help that she might have been in another world.

She looked down, and her fear was even intensified, for below her, and not very far below, was the coastline of France which, as she watched it, slipped away from her, leaving only the sea. She cast a glance at the globe above her. Already it had lost its firm circularity, was becoming flabby. No question of reaching the other side of that strip of water which had seemed so slender from their proud height. From this position it was a daunting ocean, and the waves leaped towards her, as though licking at a meal they hoped soon to enjoy.

The car took to the sea lightly enough, there being sufficient gas still to keep the balloon from complete collapse, but the fresh-blowing wind sent it scudding over the surface, tilting it so that it was in danger of capsizing. Whether the basket would float Marie did not know. It was not buoyant enough to ride the waves, which broke over it. Dripping with water, half-drowned, she wondered how long she would be able to hold on. Looking desperately for some means of easing her situation, she saw the guide-rope, and managed to throw it overboard. The heavy wet rope trailing behind steadied the car somewhat, but Marie had no hope of being able to stay afloat indefinitely. The balloon was a poor dying thing. Soon it would touch the water, and the sodden material with its intricate ropes would disappear beneath the waves, taking the car with it.

It was foolish to hope, Marie thought. She remembered the dangers she had survived, the wretchedness and loneliness of much of her girlhood. Some would say she had not had a happy life, and yet it was as precious to her as if it had been a very paradise.

When the lifeboat reached her, the car had turned over and was sinking, and still she was clinging to it. The rest of the journey was little more than a dream of food and drink, a hot bath, a warm bed, kindness from her rescuers, and on the following morning a drive back to Rye.

So near had she been to death that it took time before the everyday things of the world assumed their normal importance. As she drove through the Sussex countryside she thought of Alain, and shuddered at the thought. How could she bear to see him again, to speak to him? Then she thought of Jenkin, and began to cry. Without Jenkin the world was grey and empty.

Blanche came out when she heard the carriage approaching, and stood white and stiff. For a few moments she did not speak, and then she said, "Thank God you are alive!"

Marie could not contain her anger. "You sent Alain to Dead Man's Lane, knowing there would be trouble. You saw them preparing the balloon. Did you plan my murder together, you and Alain, as you planned my marriage?"

Blanche shook her head. "I thought Alain would take the treasure and go, but by himself. When the men told me he had taken you, and that you had seemed unwilling, I was afraid something terrible would happen, and I sent a message for the lifeboat to go out and search. I wrote down the route, from the direction of the wind, and Jenkin calculated what would happen if the wind should change."

"Jenkin? Jenkin isn't—Jenkin is not—he can't be—" She could not bring herself to say it. To speak of him as alive would be to raise hope unendurably.

"He is upstairs, in bed. I had him brought here. After all, there really was not anywhere else for him to go."

Marie missed the last sentence entirely. She was through the door and across the hall and up the stairs without realising she had moved.

When he saw her, Jenkin smiled shame-facedly. "Don't know why I always end up here. Sorry to be such a bother."

"I thought you were dead." She could say the word now, now that it was no more than a fast-fading nightmare.

"It's my shoulder again," Jenkin said, apologetically. "It always seems to get in the way when people aim at my head."

She was laughing and crying, and she went closer to him, shyly, and then suddenly her shyness wanished, and he gave a sharp cry and reminded her that he had been shot even though his heart was untouched—well, untouched in that way.

It was on the following morning that Blanche came to them and told them of Alain's death. She was drawn and haggard, but composed, accepting what was inevitable.

"When the wind changed, the basket was flung from side to side so violently that the parachute collapsed. He did not suffer. He was killed instantly. They found the jewels and the money upon him."

They were all silent for several minutes. There seemed nothing to say. But eventually Blanche bestirred herself, and took a deep breath. "When the treasure arrives you shall have it, Marie. You have a right to it."

"I don't want it. It's unlucky."

"That is a foolish and superstitious attitude," Blanche said, severely.

"All right. I don't really mind, so long as Jenkin has enough for buying his farm."

Blanche turned to leave the room, then paused. "There's one more thing. I want to give you your mother's marriage certificate. My mother stole it, and when she was dying she confessed, and gave it to me."

"She doesn't want it," Jenkin said, sharply. "She hasn't any hankering to be a de Vaudelet, and no more have I."

"Names don't mean much," Marie agreed. "Anyway, I've got four Christian names, and once I didn't have any. I was called Child, and I thought that was the only name I had."

Jenkin took her hand. "Yes, and now you've got another name. I shall call you Woman."